I want the gold.

The Olympic Flame was lit, and the crowd roared. I could imagine the cheers spreading like waves across the globe, binding us all together. For that one moment, it was hard to believe that there could ever be wars, that young people like us would ever have to fight and die instead of just competing for glory.

Later that night as I tried to drop off to sleep inside the Olympic Village, I did what I always do before a major competition. I mentally go through each routine at least twice, every move, imagining everything done perfectly. I tried to tell myself, "You've done these routines a thousand times; it's just a matter of doing them one more time." But I knew this time was different. Everybody always remembers who won the gold at the Olympics. That's the name that goes down in history. The others are forgotten. I wanted the gold.

**Look for these and other books
in THE GYMNASTS series:**

THE GYMNASTS

GO FOR THE GOLD

Elizabeth Levy

AN
APPLE
PAPERBACK

SCHOLASTIC INC.
New York Toronto London Auckland Sydney

ISBN 0-590-45253-3

12 11 10 9 8 7 6 5 4 3 2 1   2 3 4 5 6 7/9

Printed in the U.S.A.   28

First Scholastic printing, June 1992

To Jean, Dona, Monique,
and everyone at Scholastic
who believed in THE GYMNASTS
and helped them go for the gold.

Takeoff

I don't hate flying. I hate waiting to fly. My absolute least favorite place to be is buckled into a seat on an airplane that isn't going anywhere. My plane sat on the runway in the fog of San Francisco. We were waiting to take off for Denver. I wanted to be home. If the plane didn't take off soon, I'd scream.

I could just see the headlines: *HEIDI FER-GUSON — U.S. NATIONAL CHAMPION, AMER-ICA'S BEST HOPE IN OLYMPICS — GOES BER-SERK!*

"Vhy you fidget?" asked Dimitri Vickorskoff, my coach. Dimitri is a tall man, and he sat in the aisle seat with his legs stretched out. He wore cowboy boots. He's the original Hungarian cowboy. Ever since he landed in Denver, without much money and no job, he thinks that anything cowboy is good luck.

I can't argue with his reasoning. Dimitri has been good luck for me, although I wouldn't say it's all luck. Dimitri works me like a son-of-a-gun. Luck comes only to those who work hard — or, as Dimitri would say, "vork" hard. Perfect is never enough for Dimitri. It's always "von more time."

I stretched in my cramped airline seat, almost bumping my mother, who sat next to me in the window seat. Mom frowned. "I told you we should have flown first class," she said. "You are so silly sometimes about money." My father had flown back first class on an earlier flight. He's a lawyer whose first love is golf. He plays in tournaments all over the world. He is almost as good as some of the pros. He had a tournament he had to get back to.

I hadn't wanted to fly first class because I was embarrassed that my family has so much more money than most of the other girls trying out for the American Olympic team. Besides, first class had seemed like a waste of money.

I didn't want anybody to write that I had been able to pay my way to the top. However, now that we were cramped three abreast in an airplane that was sitting on the runway like a stupid fat goose, I had to admit that Mom might have been right.

"Okay, okay," I said. "When we go to the Olympics, it'll be first class."

"Guud," said Dimitri, who overheard me.

"I thought you were the one who said that money doesn't count."

"Money counts," said Dimitri. "A nickel, a dime, a quarter, mucho dollars!" He nudged me with an elbow. "That's a joke in English, yes?"

"It's a joke," I muttered. "Not a very good one." I closed my eyes and pretended to sleep. I couldn't wait to get back to my own gym and my own friends, the Pinecones.

I wish the Pinecones could have come to San Francisco to the nationals. I know they watched me on TV because they called every night to tell me how great I was.

The Pinecones are an intermediate team that work out at my home gym, the Evergreen Gymnastics Academy. Everybody who's anybody in the international gymnastics world thinks that I'm weird because I've kind of adopted the Pinecones as my home team. They are far from world-class, but they're fun.

I was glad I had done well in San Francisco. I had gotten the highest score, and I was the first picked for the U.S. team. I was relieved it was over. It had been a little depressing because the

U.S. team was just not very good this year. Chloe Chow, the best American gymnast, had suffered a stress fracture, and she wouldn't be able to compete in the Olympics. She would have been my main competition. As it stood now, the Americans didn't really have much of a chance for any medal. Except for me. I wanted a medal.

I scrunched down in my seat, trying to pick up my knapsack from beneath the seat in front of me.

"What are you doing?" complained my mother.

"I want my magazine," I said.

"Here," said Mom. "You can look at this until we take off." Mom handed me a scrapbook. She smiled. "I've decided to put everything about you in here for this Olympic year. It's something you can pass down to your children."

"What about the articles about me and anorexia and bulimia?" I asked Mom.

"Oh, Heidi," sighed Mom. "Why would you want to keep any of *those*?"

"Because those stories tell the truth," I blurted out. Mom gave me a worried look. Mom doesn't like to talk about my disease. It took me a long time to admit that I really had what they call an eating disorder. I thought I was just making sure that I looked good as a gymnast. I would eat and then make myself throw up, and I thought it was just part of my training. I didn't realize that I was making myself weaker and weaker, until finally I had to give up competing. Journalists wrote stories that I was gone for good.

But I wasn't. The truth is that I love to compete. I found out that I loved competing enough to make myself well again. I've had a lot of help. I go to my shrink, Dr. Joe List, every week when I'm back in Denver.

I still have to fight the urge to look in the mirror and think that I'm too fat when it's really muscle. Dimitri and Dr. Joe have tried to convince me that muscular is more attractive than skinny. I have never been as strong as I am right now: I can bench press twice my weight, and I can do one-arm push-ups. I am an animal. And my competitors know it. It's fun to have everybody afraid of what new trick you're going to master next.

"Heidi," said Mom. "I don't like those stories that talk about how sick you were." She sounded so defensive.

"It's okay, Mom," I said. My shrink has been trying to get me to be more tolerant of my mom and to see things from her point of view. He says that it doesn't do me any good to blame her all the time.

I took a look at Mom's scrapbook.

It was filled with box scores from the newspapers showing the preliminary events and where I stood. Mom had highlighted my name with a yellow marker. Then there was the article that showed me with the trophy.

HEIDI FERGUSON COMES BACK
UNITED STATES' ONLY HOPE

Heidi Ferguson is the new national champion. After taking the gymnastics world by storm two years ago, Heidi Ferguson was counted out when it was discovered that she had the eating disorders, anorexia and bulimia. At a little-known gym in Colorado, the Spruce Tree Gymnastics Academy, she began quietly working out. Dimitri Vickerskoff discovered her there and has masterminded her sensational comeback.

"The Spruce Tree Gymnastics Academy!" I read aloud.

Dimitri giggled. It's quite something to hear a big man giggle. "Vait till Patrick reads that," said Dimitri.

Patrick is the owner of the *Evergreen* Gymnastics Academy. It's not the Spruce Tree. Once you've had to read stories about yourself in the press, it's hard to believe anything you read in the newspapers. They get so much of it wrong, and even when they don't get it wrong, it always sounds as if they're talking about somebody you don't know.

"I miss Patrick," I said to Mom.

Dimitri grunted. "He's guud man, guud for you."

Mom bit her lip. I knew she was trying not to say anything against Patrick because she knew it would start a fight. Mom thought that Patrick wasn't experienced enough to coach me, and she thought that Dimitri was a hothead. If she had her way I'd be back in the regimented gym in California with the coach who had always wanted me "just a tiny bit thinner, more fit." I had seen my old coach at the nationals, and I had loved getting the chance to beat the gymnast she had trained.

One of her girls, Linda Offenbach, was going to the Olympics, but only as an alternate. I know for a fact that she makes herself throw up and takes laxatives to lose weight. I've told her that she's stupid to do it, but she thinks I'm just trying to sabotage her.

Mom took the scrapbook and looked at it herself. "I wish every article didn't have to mention anorexia," she said.

"They'll stop doing that when she's a vinner," said Dimitri. "At the Olympics the big story . . . the gold — that's the von!"

I grinned at Dimitri. The gold medal. Every little kid who ever goes up on a balance beam always dreams about it. Only one person ever gets it in each Olympic event. I wondered if I had a chance.

"We have now been cleared for takeoff," said the pilot. "Would the flight crew please take their seats?"

I checked my seatbelt and the button on my seat to make sure that it was upright.

I did this before the flight attendant made her announcement. Then, when her voice came over the loudspeaker, I checked it again. I just always like to check things twice. I was ready for takeoff.

2

Sometimes I'd Like to Strangle My Brother

There is nothing like working out in your home gym: no reporters waiting to ask you stupid questions, no young gymnasts who don't know you from a hole in the wall asking you for your autograph. I always feel ridiculous signing autographs. Some of the top gymnasts love it, but I don't.

I woke up in the morning, eager to get to the gym. After the hoopla of the nationals, I was more than ready for a little peace and quiet. I put on an old unitard. The tights had holes in them. I grabbed an Evergreen Gymnastics Academy T-shirt, white with the green pine tree emblem. The white had turned to yellow from all the times I had gotten it sweaty. But it was clean, so I pulled it on. I liked the fact that it was extra large and droopy. It had been washed so many times that the cotton was as soft as a baby blanket. It's one of my favorite T-shirts.

It was hot outside, so I didn't bother putting jeans on over my tights.

"I'm ready to go!" I yelled.

My younger brother Chris was standing by the station wagon. Chris is just a year younger than I am. He's almost fourteen, and he's a great free-style skier, a real daredevil. Normally, he dresses in baggy shorts and T-shirts. Today, he was dressed in a short-sleeved shirt and clean and pressed khakis.

"Where are you going?" I asked him. "You look like you're applying for a summer job."

"Uh, I'm going to the gym, too," he said. Chris doesn't do gymnastics, but he sometimes uses the equipment in my gym for his ski conditioning, particularly the trampoline.

Guys with great muscles like Chris should never wear those nerdy short-sleeved shirts. I decided I'd better tell him. "Chris, much as Darlene likes clothes, I don't think she needs to see you looking like a dork." Darlene and Chris are kind of an item.

Darlene Broderick is one of the oldest kids on the Pinecone team, and she's one of their best athletes. If she'd ever take gymnastics seriously, she could be really good. Her father is "Big Beef" Broderick, the football player for the Denver Broncos.

"Hey, at least I look presentable," said Chris. "You look like a slob. You're not wearing that to the gym, are you?"

I stared at him. "Since when do you care how I dress for the gym?"

Mom came out of the house with the car keys in her hand. I started to climb into the backseat.

"Heidi," said Mom, "your tights have holes in them. Go change."

"See?" said Chris, raising his eyebrows.

"Will you two stop worrying about how I look? Nobody's going to be taking my picture. Leave me alone."

I have a voice I use that everybody knows means business. Even my mom doesn't mess with me when I use that voice.

Mom put on her seat belt. "Suit yourself," she said with a sigh. Mom sighs a lot under normal circumstances.

I relaxed as we turned onto the road past the Evergreen Mall. "Wherever I wander," I warbled, "there's no place like home. . . ."

Chris put his hands over his ears. "You have the worst singing voice in the entire universe," he said.

"I am tone deaf," I admitted. "I'm just glad to be back."

The Evergreen Gymnastics Academy is a converted warehouse on the road behind the mall. From the outside it's just a gray cement building, but on the inside, I knew I would find my friends, my equipment, and my coaches.

I stretched my arms in front of me and rolled my shoulders up toward my ears, loosening up.

Chris turned around in the front seat. "That T-shirt looks yucky," he said.

"Enough about her clothes, Chris," said Mom. I was surprised. Mom usually cares about appearances more than anybody. It was a nice change to hear her not worried about the way I looked.

"Thanks, Mom," I said, as we pulled up in front of the gym. I'd have to remember to tell Dr. Joe that Mom had actually said something decent.

I got out of the car. Mom opened the car door and got out.

"Uh, Mom," I asked, "why are you getting out of the car?"

Mom and Chris glanced at each other. "I have to pay Patrick for your lessons."

I shrugged, but I was unaccountably annoyed. Sometimes I get in these moods when I'm just jumpy. Often it happens after a big meet, when I've been in the spotlight too long. I feel as if I

12

can't concentrate and that nothing is going right. The only cure is to work out. I needed some down time, some quiet time.

I didn't want Mom or even Chris in the gym. I wanted to see my friends, say hello, and get back to work.

"Why don't you give *me* the check for Patrick? I'll bet you're tired. You probably have jet lag."

"Jet lag!" hooted Chris. "It's an hour's difference between California and here. Mom doesn't have jet lag."

Sometimes I'd like to strangle my brother. My brother and mom followed me into the gym.

3

Lopsided Gold Rings

"SURPRISE!" I heard the shout before it registered. I didn't even get a chance to put down my gym bag.

I did a double take. The Pinecones — Lauren Baca, Jodi Sutton, Cindi Jockett, Ti An Truong, Ashley Frank, and Darlene Broderick — were standing in the center of the gym. Each one was holding a large golden ring made out of painted pinecones.

A big computer paper banner was stretched across the gym. WELCOME HOME, CHAMPION! Patrick and Dimitri beamed at me. I looked around the gym. I couldn't believe it. Every gymnast in all of Denver seemed to be there. I saw kids from the Atomic Amazons gym in downtown Denver, and the Grandstanders and their coach from Littleton, Colorado. The gym was packed.

I closed my eyes, hoping it would all go away.

"She's so surprised. She's in shock," I heard Ti An say. Ti An is one of the youngest gymnasts, and she takes everything very seriously.

"It's a proven fact that being surprised can rush all the blood from your head," said Lauren. "If you're going to faint, put your head between your knees." Lauren always says "it's a proven fact . . ."

"You'll make us look pretty stupid if you faint," whispered Jodi. "We've been working on this surprise party for a month."

"I told you it might not be a good idea," said Ashley. Ashley's a twerp.

I started to giggle. It was almost a hysterical laugh. I hiccuped.

"Oh, goodie," said Jodi. "She's so happy she burped. I'm glad we got that on videotape."

I looked up alarmed. There was Becky Dyson with a video recorder pressed to her eye.

"Becky, put that down," I commanded her.

Becky lowered the camera. "I told the Pinecones that a surprise party is so juvenile," said Becky.

Becky is not exactly a model of maturity, although she likes to think that she is. She is a better gymnast than the Pinecones, and she thinks that makes her a better person. Actually, the Pinecones have been improving while Becky has been standing still. She's one of those athletes who start out with natural talent and then get stuck on being told how good they are. She's never learned how to put in the real sweat that makes a champion.

Everyone thinks that I was born with so much natural ability and that it all comes easy to me. There are a lot of gymnasts out there with more natural grace than I. But nobody works harder than I do.

I went over to Patrick. He's young to be the owner of a gym, and he's cute. He gave me a hug.

"Congratulations, champion," he said.

"She's National Champion, not Olympic Champion, yet," said Dimitri. "At the Olympics ve find out who's really champion. The nationals vere just a piece of pizza."

"Piece of cake," I corrected him.

"Ve celebrate vith cake *after* the Olympics, not before."

"Don't be a spoilsport, Dimitri," warned Patrick.

"I did worry that a surprise party would be too much for you, after all the excitement of San Francisco," said Mom.

Chris rolled his eyes. "Heidi's not a piece of

fragile china," he said. "This is supposed to be *fun*."

"Dimitri and your mom didn't think this party was such a good idea," said Patrick. "But the Pinecones had their hearts set on it. I didn't want to disappoint them. You don't mind, do you?"

The Pinecones were standing a respectful distance away from us, looking worried.

"No," I lied, "of course not."

"You have to remain focused from now until the Olympics. You have only six weeks to get ready," said Mom.

"For vonce, your mom and I agree," said Dimitri.

I glanced over at the Pinecones. "On the other hand, I didn't have anybody to celebrate with in San Francisco."

My mom looked hurt.

"Uh, I just meant that I missed the Pinecones," I said quickly.

Dimitri laughed. He clapped Mom on the back. "The kids . . . they always love to be vith their own." He brought a glass of punch over to Mom. "Go, Heidi, have fun. Tomorrow ve vork our kneecaps off."

"It's *tails* off, Dimitri," I said.

"I told them that they should keep the party very low-key. We don't want you to get overexcited," said Mom. She was beginning to repeat herself.

"Mom," I frowned, "the Pinecones are not going to get me overexcited."

"You never know what could trigger a bad reaction in you," said Mom.

I rolled my eyes. I wanted out of there. I could use some company around my own age.

The Pinecones were standing in a bunch, hopping from one foot to the other. I skipped over to join them. Darlene looked worried. "We heard that Dimitri thought we shouldn't be having a party."

"I didn't think it was a good idea," said Becky, sidling over.

I certainly wasn't going to give Becky the satisfaction of putting down the Pinecones. "It was a great idea," I said. I looked around the gym. "Why did you invite the Amazons?"

I knew the Pinecones hated the Amazons.

"It's a proven fact that we *love* to make them jealous," said Lauren. "And they're jealous that even an honorary Pinecone is going to the Olympics."

I grinned at her. I was *not* going to be a spoilsport at my own party.

"We've got punch and cake," said Ti An.

"Heidi might not eat cake," said Becky. She

mouthed the word *anorexia* as if I couldn't read lips.

Jodi glared at her. "Becky, you remind me of a carpet."

"What's that supposed to mean?" demanded Becky.

"You're just so tacky," said Jodi.

"Tacky!" screeched Becky. "At least I didn't make lopsided rings."

"They aren't lopsided!" yelled Cindi. "It's just that some of the pinecones fell off."

I looked at the welcome-home banner and the five gold rings that the pinecones had been holding. They were leaning against the wall by the refreshment table. Several of the spray-painted pinecones had fallen off and were scattered on the floor.

"We got gold paint all over ourselves," said Jodi. "We looked like something from that old James Bond movie."

"The pinecones wouldn't stick," said Ti An sadly. "Patrick wouldn't let us use instant glue. He was worried that we'd get our fingers stuck together."

"I think those pinecone rings are terrific," I said to Ti An.

"You can take one home," said Lauren.

"She wants to bring home a gold medal," said

Becky. "She doesn't want a gold pinecone ring."

"I want them both," I said.

"That's so stupid," muttered Becky. "You're just indulging them."

"Becky," I said. "Get your video camera out. I want a picture of me with all the Pinecones, right in front of those rings."

"Maybe we can stand in front of the missing pinecones and cover them up," said Ti An.

"No," I said. "I want them just the way they are."

I Love Being a Bug

I finally got my wish. The gym was quiet, a little too quiet. I had twice-a-day full-out work-outs. I worked with Dimitri from eight in the morning until twelve. Then I had a lunch break, and I studied the diagrams of my moves. Dimitri had designed a new vault for me, so that we would have something to surprise the judges with. I was adding a full twist to my layout, after doing a roundoff onto the vault. Only one person in the world could do that vault: Nadia Maleno-vich, the great Russian gymnast. Everybody assumed that she had a lock on the gold. She had been world champion a record four times in a row.

After my lunch break, I went back to the gym

and worked out until six at night. This was when the Pinecones were also doing their workouts, and it should have been the time that was the most fun. It wasn't. I had been following this routine for two weeks, and the Pinecones were giving me the silent treatment.

I was working out on the trampoline when the Pinecones filed in from the locker room to begin their warm-ups. Darlene gave a little wave, but she didn't stop to talk the way she usually did. Ti An and Ashley went straight to the mats and began their stretching. Jodi, Lauren, and Cindi walked right by the trampoline, hardly glancing at me.

"Hi-ya, Jodi-podi!" I shouted from the height of my jump. I love the trampoline. I wish it were an Olympic event. It is so much fun to just fly.

Jodi looked up and gave me a kind of shy wave. She looked a little embarrassed. I felt bad. Maybe I had hurt her feelings, using the nickname that her stepbrother teases her with. But I thought she'd know that I meant it affectionately. I was just trying to break the ice.

I signaled to Dimitri that I needed to take a break.

"Vhat's up?" he asked.

"Give me a minute," I said.

Dimitri scowled, but I had been working my butt off for the past two weeks, and he knew it.

"Okay, okay," he said. "A three-minute break."

"Five minutes," I said. "And then I'll do something that will knock your socks off."

Dimitri nodded. I grabbed the side of the trampoline and somersaulted to the floor.

"Hey, guys!" I shouted.

Jodi, Lauren, and Cindi turned around.

"Hi, Heidi-ho," said Lauren. The other two gave Lauren a dirty look as if she had said something wrong, but I was used to stupid puns on my name, like "Heidi-seek," and so on. At least Lauren was smiling. The others were giving me the cold shoulder.

"Whoops, I'd better go warm up," said Lauren. She took off like a scared rabbit, leaving me with Cindi and Jodi. Lauren ran to the far end of the gym where Ti An and Ashley were stretching on the bars.

"Hi, Cindi," I said. Cindi blushed so that her face matched her red hair, and all I had done was say hello. Jodi just looked at the floor as if there were an anthill down there and she was a scientist.

"Jodi?"

Jodi lifted her head. I couldn't read the expression in her blue eyes, and usually Jodi is the easiest person in the world to read. Whatever she's feeling instantly shows in her face.

"Is anything wrong, guys?" I asked them.

23

Jodi and Cindi both shook their heads. "No," said Jodi, but her voice cracked. "Why, what could be wrong?"

"You're not mad at me for calling you Jodi-podi, are you?" I asked her. "You know I didn't mean it like your brother, Nick the Pest, does. I just wanted to get your attention."

Jodi shrugged. I was worried that I had really hurt her feelings.

"Forget it," said Jodi. She gave me a weak smile.

"Do you guys want to watch me on the trampoline?" I asked. "I'm going to do something that will wow Dimitri."

"Sure," said Cindi.

Jodi put her hand on Cindi's arm. "Uh, I think we'd better go warm up," she said. She cocked her chin toward the far end of the floor where the rest of the Pinecones were doing their stretches.

"Well, okay," I said, but I felt kind of funny, as if I had been pushy asking them to come watch me. Usually the Pinecones love to watch. Maybe I do show off a little in front of them, but it had always seemed harmless before.

I just couldn't figure out where and when they had gotten this attitude toward me.

I walked back to Dimitri. "So, young lady, you vant to knock my mittens off?"

"Socks off," I said. Although Dimitri might be a genius about gymnastics, he certainly can mangle the English language. But then, as he points out, *I* don't speak Hungarian, Russian, or French, three languages that Dimitri speaks fluently.

"Dimitri," I asked, "did I do anything to insult the Pinecones?"

"Insult?" he asked.

"You know, snub them or make them mad or something."

"I know what insult means," said Dimitri, drawing up to his full six feet four inches. Dimitri can be a little touchy about his English. "Vhy you vorry about the Pinecones? You vorry about Nadia Malenovich. She gives you plenty to vorry about."

He was right, of course.

I climbed back onto the trampoline and began my jumps. With each rebound I went higher and higher. A few months ago, when I was working on my double-somersault dismount from the bars, I had overrotated and ended up doing a triple. Nobody has ever done a triple somersault as a dismount.

I waited until I could time my rebound for the moment I was at the highest, then I went into a tuck. I threw my weight down toward my head, grabbing my knees to keep my body in a tight ball. I somersaulted, once, twice, three times, then I straightened my legs, hit the trampoline, jumped up again to the exact same height and did it again, perfectly. I landed and looked over at Dimitri and gave him a big grin.

When I said that I am not blessed with the most natural talent of any gymnast who ever lived, I wasn't exactly telling the truth. I do have an almost extrasensory ability to find my bearings in space. This means that when I'm in tight spin, I can always tell exactly where the floor is, and I don't get dizzy or nauseated. I would probably make a great astronaut.

Dimitri had his hands on his hips. He threw back his head and laughed. "Twice in a row!" he exclaimed.

"And you thought the first time I did it, it was a mistake," I said. "Remember before the nationals, I did it on the bars, but you insisted I put it away and concentrate on my routine for the meet. Well, I want to add it to my routine for the Olympics. I know I'm ready. For real."

Dimitri looked doubtful. "The bars are not the trampoline."

"I know," I said. "But I've been testing it out. I've been trying to do it from the trampoline a little lower than from the bars. I'll have more room to do it from the high bar. Come on. Let me show you."

I grabbed Dimitri's hand and dragged him over to the uneven bars.

"My little bug, she's always thinking," said Dimitri.

I grinned at him. Dimitri's highest compliment is to call me a bug.

I loved being a bug.

5

I Hate Gushers

The Pinecones were standing around the uneven bars. Patrick had a clipboard in his hand, and he was diagramming a new move for them.

I waited by the chalk bin. There were none of the usual Pinecone jokes when they saw me. Instead, they ignored me. I wondered what I had done to get them mad at me. I couldn't think of anything.

Patrick looked up when he saw me. At least he smiled. "What's up?" he asked.

"Nothing," I said. "When you're finished with the bars, I want to try something." It was a little awkward being the star in the gym. In this last month before the Olympics, basically I had free run of the gym. If I had said, "Patrick, I need the bars," he would have moved the Pinecones for me. So I didn't want to say it.

"We're just about done here," said Patrick. "Besides, the Pinecones can probably learn more from watching you than from any of my diagrams, right?"

Darlene was studying a crack in the mats that she was standing on. She shrugged. Darlene is the captain of the Pinecones, and her shrug seemed to speak for all of them. None of them would look at me.

"The little bug thinks she do the triple for a dismount," said Dimitri.

"Remember months ago, before the nationals, when I did a triple on the trampoline by mistake?" I explained to the Pinecones. I had decided that one of us had to act normally, and it would be me.

Lauren nodded. Her eyes looked bright. "Yeah, it was amazing."

The other Pinecones stared at her as if she had said something wrong. Lauren quickly looked away, and her eyes got cloudy.

I tried to shrug it off. "Anyhow, I've been doing it consistently on the trampoline, and I want to try it." My voice sounded clipped and angry, and I didn't try to hide it. Why were the Pinecones picking this time of all times to get into a snit? I didn't need any distractions right before the Olympics.

I shook my shoulders and went over to the chalk bin and dipped my hands in. I was careful to make sure that I had chalk up and down my wrists and on my leather grips. It might look messy, but I knew that the extra chalk might just give me the extra grasp that I needed. I checked my handgrips twice.

Becky was standing by the chalk bin. "Oh, Heidi," she gushed, "you looked so spectacular on the trampoline."

I hate gushers.

"Thanks," I muttered. I walked away.

"I can't wait until we go to the Olympics!" Becky shouted after me.

I saw the Pinecones all lift their heads. Becky has one of those piercing voices that really carries.

I turned around. "What do you mean 'we'?" I asked.

"Oh, I've had tickets reserved for years," she said. "My parents are taking me. We're staying at the best hotel."

"Great," I muttered.

"So I don't have to watch you now," said Becky. "I'll see so much of you there. We can have dinner. It'll give you a chance to relax."

"Becky," I said in my warning voice, "relaxing is not why I'm going to the Olympics."

Becky just grinned at me. I knew that I could insult her to her face and she would still smile and take it. That's the problem with being a star: The idiots want to be your friends, and your real friends treat you as if you're a stranger.

I went to the bars. At least the bars were familiar and friendly. I knew every nuance of their bends and creaks. Up on the bars, I didn't have to worry about anybody except myself.

I wasn't planning on doing my entire bar routine, but I felt good up there — I didn't want to come down. I did a few giant circles over the high bar and then beat down against the lower bar. The momentum carried me ever higher. Doing well on bars is as much a quality of rhythm as it is of upper-body strength. You can't try to overpower the bars. They'll fight you back. But if you give in to the swing and the momentum, it is like flying. You don't have to be an eagle to fly, although wing strength doesn't hurt.

I saw Dimitri watching me with his arms crossed over his chest. His dark eyes were hooded like a hawk's.

I'd have to get off this bird kick. Usually I don't have time to think, but today I just loved the freedom. Nobody to worry about except myself.

At the height of my last giant circle, I let go of

the bars, I was at least twelve feet or higher above the mats. I threw my body into a tight tuck, letting myself spin around. I didn't have time to worry about where I was in relation to the ground; the speed of my turns made the ground irrelevant for the moment.

Then I stretched out my legs, pointed my toes, and hit the mats with a thud. No bird ever landed like that. The power of my turns threw me forward with the force of a freight train, but I fought back. It wasn't pretty, but I didn't take a step or fall to my knees. I stuck the landing.

"Oh, wow! Absolutely incredible!" chirped a high-pitched voice. Becky ran over to me. She gave me a hug. I held my arms to the side and didn't hug her back.

"That was so spectacular!" Becky bubbled. "You are the only one in the world who could ever do it." She tried to hug me again.

The Pinecones just gaped at Becky. Becky turned and glared at them.

"What are you goofs staring at?" she demanded. "I'm Heidi's cheering section. I'll be at Barcelona. You won't."

"Becky," warned Patrick, "that's enough. Leave Heidi alone. I'm sure Dimitri wants to talk to her." Patrick clapped me on the back. "That was something else, Heidi," he said.

"Thanks," I said. Praise from Patrick, I enjoyed. Patrick wasn't a gusher.

Dimitri was stroking his moustache. "The landing," he said. "You look like turkey falling from sky. No guud."

I heard a giggle. It was Lauren. The other Pinecones shushed her.

Dimitri grabbed Patrick's clipboard. "Here," he said. "If you time the release a split second before, you gain an extra six inches or a foot — that gives you time to stretch out. If you're going to try this — and no promises — but maybe, just maybe ve can do it — it has to be perfect."

It was strange with Dimitri's English. Some of the time I can hardly understand a word he's saying. Then when he really gets serious, it's as if he's been speaking English all his life.

"Okay, so you vant to do this. Ve do it again."

"Von more time!" I said. I looked around for the Pinecones. Ordinarily, they would have laughed with me, but not now.

Becky overheard me and nodded eagerly. I turned my back on her and looked down at the diagram that Dimitri had made for me.

I didn't have time to worry about the Pinecones. I had vork to do.

6

A Lot to Talk About

"Here we have Heidi Ferguson. Heidi, we understand that you owe everything to your brother. Is that true?" Chris had balled his hand into a fist and was pretending to talk into a microphone.

I made a face at him. "Apparently, Heidi Ferguson has her face permanently frozen into an ugly puss. We'll go on to the beautiful Nadia Malenovich." Chris stuck out his tongue at me. He poured out a huge bowl of cereal and cut a banana into it.

"Chris," said my dad, "don't tease your sister."

"Who's teasing?" insisted Chris. "Heidi's been practicing like a mad dog for the Olympics, and she's forgetting to practice the one skill she'll need."

"And what's that, oh Wise One?" I asked, pouring out my own bowl of cereal, not that much smaller than Chris's.

"Talking to reporters. For example, if one saw you eating breakfast, he'd say, "Ferguson, you eat only cereal. It looks like birdseed. Are you still fighting your dramatic battle with anorexia?"

My father started to smile. "Chris!" shrieked my mother. "You can't make jokes about that. Cut that out!"

My father's smile left his face. "I've got to be going," he said. "I've got to go to the office." My father is a lawyer, and I know he works hard, but he also likes to duck out of any family fights. He stood up and gave me a kiss.

He turned to my mother. "Chris is right, you know. Heidi does need practice handling the media. They're bound to be all over her in Barcelona."

"I can handle the media," said my mother. "I've got it all planned out. I'm going to hire a specialist."

"Who?" I asked.

"Marshall Marshak," answered my mother. "He's supposed to be the best sports agent in the business. He operates out of New York."

"With a name like Marshall Marshak, he'd better be good," said Chris.

Dad frowned. "I've heard about him," he said. "He's supposed to be excellent, but a little bit of a shark."

"It'll be good to have a shark on our side," said my mother. "We'll have to sort through all the endorsement offers. We'll need somebody handling the media for us."

"I thought that I would be the one helping Heidi with that stuff," said my dad. "I can negotiate contracts for endorsements."

Mom sniffed. "Right, and then the first call from your office or golf tournament, and you'll have other priorities."

"Does anybody want *my* opinion about any of this?" I said irritably.

Chris winked at me. "No," he mouthed.

I rolled my eyes. Mom followed Dad out into the living room arguing about whether or not I needed an agent. I listened to them for a minute.

"I'm not sure that I want anybody 'handling' me," I moaned to Chris. "I've already got too many adults in my life as it is."

"Relax," said Chris. "Maybe this Marshall character will keep Mom off your back."

Chris is younger than I, but sometimes he

is really smart about people. A lot of the things about Mom and Dad that literally almost drive me crazy just roll off Chris's back.

"Hey, Chris, can I ask you something?" I asked.

"That's the stupidest question. I don't know why people say that. You know I'm going to say yes, then if it's a question I don't want to answer, I'm stuck. Just ask it."

"Has Darlene talked to you about me?" I asked.

"O Great One, the entire world is talking about you. Nobody can ever think of a single other subject of conversation. We try to think of other things to talk about, but you are just so fascinating — "

"Shut up," I said to him. "I'm serious. There's enough weirdness in my life this month, and now the Pinecones have been acting peculiar. They hardly talk to me. I'm worried that they're hurt because I didn't act excited enough about their surprise party. So has Darlene mentioned that the Pinecones are mad at me?"

Chris shook his head. "You got it all wrong," he said. "They're trying to be good. They think that you need them to disappear in order for you to stay focused on the Olympics."

"What?" I exclaimed. "Who gave them that idea?"

Chris cocked his head toward the front hall where he could hear Mom and Dad arguing. "Three guesses," he said.

"Darn her."

"Mom didn't want them to have the surprise party. She thought you wouldn't want all that excitement after the stress of the nationals. She told them that afterward they'd have to lay off you, leave you alone, that you don't need any aggravation."

"She's the aggravation. Why does she always have to butt in?"

"Hey," said Chris, "she was only trying to help."

I scowled at him. "In her way," Chris added.

Mom walked back into the kitchen. "Well," she said brightly, "your father agrees with me. We do need the best for you. You'll get a chance to meet Marshall Marshak in Barcelona. He'll be there. He's representing some of the top athletes in track and field, too."

"Mom," I said, "forget about that Marshall character for a moment. I want to talk to you."

"Oh," said Mom. I could see her shoulders tense. She recognized my tone of voice.

"Look, I don't like you interfering with my friendships. You had no right to tell the Pine-cones that they had to disappear."

Chris pretended to be counting the Cheerios in his bowl.

"The Pinecones have been acting as if they wouldn't touch me with a ten-foot pole," I complained. "And from what Chris tells me, it's all your fault for telling them to leave me alone."

"You *do* need to be left alone," argued Mom. "This Pinecone nonsense was, perhaps, something you needed when you lost your confidence, but now they are just a drag on you. With the Olympics only a few weeks away, you cannot have a single distraction. The Pinecones *are* a distraction."

I made a face. "They are the only reason I'm still *in* gymnastics," I protested.

Chris looked up from his cereal.

"I doubt that," sniffed Mom.

"Actually I doubt it, too," said Chris.

"Oh, shut up," I said.

"Hey," snapped Chris, "just 'cause you're a little tense right now does not give you the right to tell me to shut up. Quit it."

Chris had a point. "Sorry," I mumbled.

"I assume that apology is meant for me, too," said Mom.

Chris put a finger to his lips as if warning me not to push things too far. He knew exactly what I wanted to say to Mom, and that it would only get me in very hot water.

I studied my cereal with the same concentration as Chris. Well, at least I had an appointment with Dr. Joe today. I hadn't seen him since San Francisco. I knew that we'd have a lot to talk about.

7

Not Wimpy — Human

Dr. Joe was glad to see me. He gave me a huge grin. Then he saw the expression on my face.

"Sit down," he said gently. "What's up? How was San Francisco? You looked great on television, and I was thrilled when you won."

"San Francisco was terrific," I said. "It's being back home that's been the problem."

Dr. Joe sat back and waited for me to talk. When I first was told that I'd have to see a shrink for my anorexia and bulimia, I thought it meant sitting in a stuffy office and having somebody ask me personal questions all the time. I hated that idea.

But Dr. Joe turned out to be something completely different from what I expected. He doesn't

41

ask that many questions, and he's not stuffy. He doesn't look that much older than Patrick. His office is full of posters from rock concerts. He actually likes The Grateful Dead. Chris loves his office. He's come with me a couple of times for some family counseling that we did when I first started. Now, I mostly see Dr. Joe by myself.

I looked over at the fish tank that Dr. Joe has conveniently placed where patients can stare at it when they don't feel like talking. That's one of the best things about being in his office. I *don't* have to talk unless I feel like it.

I watched one of the bright neon fish dart back and forth in the underwater castle in the fish tank. The room was so quiet all I could hear was the bubbles from the tank.

"It's Mom again," I said finally. "I've been trying to give her a chance, but all she does is make me want to strangle her."

I looked up at him. "You were the one who said I should be nicer to her," I accused him.

"Nice to her, but don't let her walk all over you. What's been going on?"

I told Dr. Joe about the surprise party and the way that the Pinecones had been acting. "Now it turns out to be all Mom's fault," I said. "She told the Pinecones to give me the silent treatment. I hate it."

Dr. Joe nodded.

"At first, I thought it was the Pinecones' fault. I blamed them, because they didn't have to do what Mom said. And I felt mad at them. But it's not their fault," I blurted out. "They're just being good friends. It's all Mom's fault. She doesn't know what it is to have friends. She never did. She never will."

I crossed my arms over my chest and sunk down in the seat. I sighed. There I went again, blaming Mom, but I was really mad at her.

"I'm gonna be stuck in Barcelona with her and not them," I muttered.

"Them?" asked Dr. Joe.

"The Pinecones," I snapped. "You knew who I meant."

"Yes?"

I was really getting mad now. "What does 'yes?' mean? You know, sometimes you sound like you're not even here. You could just leave a tape recorder in the office that said, 'yes?' " I glared at him.

Dr. Joe looked at me. "What do you think is really going on with the Pinecones?"

"I'm mad at them for just doing what Mom told them to. They should have known that, right now, before the Olympics, I need them more than ever."

"Just for the Olympics?" asked Dr. Joe.

I nodded eagerly. "See, the Pinecones keep me

loose. When I was first in the hospital, I was wound so tight I thought I'd never even want to set foot in a gym again. But then I met them, and they were all so loosey-goosey and fun. They didn't treat me with kid gloves. It was just fun being around them. It was fun being back in the gym. They got me started again."

"So maybe now that you're back, you don't need them anymore," said Dr. Joe.

I stared at him. "You're sounding just like Mom," I complained. "I can't believe you'd say something like that!"

"Look, Heidi, the Pinecones are friends, not crutches."

I stared at him. "Are you saying I haven't been a good friend?" I yelled at him.

"I'd say understandably you've been preoccupied with the Olympics," said Dr. Joe.

"It's Mom who's preoccupied. She's even hired some stupid P.R. guy to take care of me in Barcelona."

"We can talk about that later. Let's stay on the subject of the Pinecones," said Dr. Joe. "Do you think you've been a good friend?"

"You're telling me that I *haven't* been a good friend," I snapped at him. "That's a lousy thing to say to somebody who's about to go to the Olympics."

44

"What does the Olympics have to do with it?" asked Dr. Joe.

"Yeah, right. The Olympics are just another meet," I said sarcastically. "Like it's not the most important event of my life. And the Pinecones won't even be there. It's not my fault that the Pinecones chose to listen to my mom instead of coming to me. The Olympics *are* the most important event of my life."

"And?"

"And the Pinecones won't be there." I blinked. The thought of being alone at the Olympics made me want to cry.

I sighed. "I've been so preoccupied with the Olympics, I've been acting like a creep. I should have been the one to ask them what was up. I never even wondered why they were avoiding me."

Dr. Joe sat back. He gets a look on his face when I finally *get* something. "Whether you win or lose, gold medal or no gold medal, you and the girls at that gym have something special going. You should let them know that means something to you."

"Yeah," I said, "especially because things are so unfair. That twerp Becky Dyson is going to the Olympics, and the Pinecones are going to have to stay at home and watch me on television.

And I'll be in Barcelona with Mom and Dad. Chris will be there, but it's not enough."

"Who do you really want there?"

"The Pinecones," I said quickly. "I really wish they were coming. I need them. They're the only ones except for Chris who can make me laugh. But it's impossible."

Dr. Joe just looked at me. Sometimes I wished he'd say more.

I bit my lip. I hadn't even told the Pinecones that I would have liked to have them come. I knew that other gymnasts sometimes take their whole gymnastic club to the Olympics. I had assumed I had to go alone with just Mom, Dad, Chris, and Dimitri.

"What are you thinking?" Dr. Joe asked me.

"What are you thinking?" I sassed him back. Dr. Joe is one adult who I can be rude to and it never gets back to my mom or dad.

I twisted my neck around. It crinkled. The muscles in my back were tight. When I had first talked about getting back into gymnastics, I had told Dr. Joe that it was impossible to ever make it back to the top. Here I was, America's best Olympic chance for a medal.

Dr. Joe coughed. "Heidi? What's up?"

"I want the Pinecones to come with me," I said.

"Good," said Dr. Joe. "I think that would be great."

I smiled at him.

"Do you really think I could swing it?" I asked.

"You'll never know unless you try," said Dr. Joe. "There are only six of them. You should be able to get them tickets. It's a lot to arrange at the last minute, but it shouldn't be impossible."

"Mom will have a cow if they all come. She'll be sure they'd be a huge distraction."

"Maybe that's just what you need," said Dr. Joe. "But remember they're friends, not crutches. You don't need them to win, but you need them as friends."

"That sounds so wimpy."

"Not wimpy — human," said Dr. Joe.

8

Bragging Rights

The locker room is a great equalizer. I can remember when I was going through my worst stage of anorexia. When I looked at myself in the mirror I could count the bones in my rib cage. I didn't see that as weird. I saw the other girls as fat, but I can remember catching sight of other gymnasts staring at me and being really grossed out. I learned to hide in one of the little alcoves.

The locker room of the Evergreen Gymnastics Academy is like everything else about the place — not at all fancy. No steam rooms, or vanities, or hair dryers. The locker room is one big room with no place to hide. There's only one mirror at the end near the showers. The rest is just low benches recently painted bright red and yellow. Patrick had decided it was time to brighten up the place.

I sat down on one of the yellow benches in between my workouts and waited for the Pinecones. Ti An was the first one in.

"Hi, Ti An," I said. "How're you doing?"

Ti An blinked at me a little shyly. Ti An is always shy, although when you get to know her she's got a wicked sense of humor. I like her. She's a good gymnast, and she's got the potential to be excellent. She has the right body for it — a long torso with short legs.

"I'm fine, fine," she said, ducking her head with every "fine." Ashley came in and grabbed her arm. I could see the two of them whispering as if Ashley were reminding Ti An not to bother me. I would have my work cut out for me talking some sense into the Pinecones. I wanted to get them all together.

It was just my luck that Becky was the next one in the locker room.

"Oh, Heidi," she exclaimed, "you look tired. Is everything all right? Of course, you must be exhausted with all the training you're doing."

I hate people who tell me I look tired when I'm working hard. Who wouldn't be tired doing two four-hour workouts a day? Get real. If Becky tried to do one quarter of what I was doing, she would drop out like a rock.

"I'm fine," I said through gritted teeth.

"Well, I've been reading about the training programs of some of the top athletes, and they say it's important to relax a little before a major event. My parents and I would love it if you would join us for lunch or dinner. My mom's already made reservations at the fanciest and most expensive restaurant in Barcelona. I can't remember what it's called — some Spanish name."

"Well, Barcelona *is* in Spain, Becky," I said, trying hard not to laugh in her face.

Becky is not known for her sense of humor. She just kept going. "It's very exclusive and hard to get into, what with all the hoopla for the Olympics, so I'm sure you'll want to come."

Sometimes Becky's stupidity actually takes my breath away. "Uh, Becky, I'm going to Barcelona to try to win a gold medal, not for a vacation."

"Yeah, but you've got to eat," persisted Becky. "And this restaurant is supposed to have the best food in town."

I looked up. The other Pinecones had arrived.

"What restaurant?" asked Darlene. "My mom and dad still think the Rattlesnake Club is the best."

"Puhl-leese, Darlene," said Becky. "I'm not talking about this cowtown. I'm talking about Europe. I'm talking about the capital of Spain."

"Oh, great, Becky," teased Lauren. "Did you

and your folks make a reservation for a restaurant in Madrid? That's a long drive for dinner. It's about five hundred miles."

"What are you talking about?"

Lauren began to giggle. "The capital of Spain is Madrid, not Barcelona," she said.

"Well, who cares?" snapped Becky. "They've got Spanish food all over that country."

Lauren, Darlene, and I started to laugh. "What's so funny?" Becky demanded.

It wasn't nice to be laughing at her, but it sure was fun.

I tried to stop myself. "Becky, thanks for the invitation, but I won't be eating any rich food while I'm over there."

"You aren't going to be watching your diet like . . . you know."

Becky seemed to think that words like *anorexia* and *bulimia* were too delicate for my ears.

"No, I won't be making myself throw up," I said. "It's just that I don't think I'll be going to any fancy restaurants until the Olympics are over."

"I understand," said Becky. She finished putting on her leotard and checked her blond curls in the mirror. Becky has the kind of cute looks that are already starting to look a little too cute. You can just tell that once she quits gymnastics, she's going to have a weight problem.

Becky fluffed out her hair. "My mom told me that I'm going to have to be careful in Europe because all the boys there have a thing for blondes."

"Becky," said Lauren, "it's a proven fact that Europe is the only place in the world except the U.S. where there *are* a lot of blondes."

I started to giggle again. I had missed all of Lauren's "proven facts."

Becky's mouth dropped open. "That can't be true," she said.

"Yeah, Becky," I said. "Blondes are a disappearing species — face it."

Darlene caught my eye, and we started to laugh together again. A lot of American gymnasts are the standard blonde — but I'm not, with my black hair and pale coloring. Darlene certainly isn't. She's black. Lauren's Hispanic. Ti An's Vietnamese. No wonder I liked hanging out with the Pinecones. I fit in. I'd have to tell them that.

"Uh, Becky," I said quickly. "I didn't mean to make fun of you. Listen, would you mind if I talked to the Pinecones alone for a minute?"

I knew that Becky was mad at me for laughing at her, but she'd never tell me off. Bullies and snobs like Becky only pick on kids who they think aren't important. They are so dense. Becky would take any amount of abuse from me, just because I was famous. She wanted to brag that she had gone "out to dinner" with Heidi Ferguson. She didn't really want my company. She just wanted bragging rights.

"Oh, sure, Heidi. I'll leave you alone with the Pinecones. After all, they won't get to see you in Barcelona, and I will," she chattered.

"Don't be so sure about that, Becky," I said.

Darlene stared at me. "How did you know?" she said. "I've been keeping it a secret."

"What secret?" I exclaimed. "I don't have a secret."

"I do," said Darlene. "But I wasn't going to tell anybody about it."

9

The Pinecones
Are My Center

"You go first," Darlene and I said in unison.

"No, you," said Darlene. "I want to hear what you've got to say."

I nodded my head. Darlene is the exact opposite of Becky. She would never let me get away with anything just because I'm a celebrated gymnast. Maybe it's because she's had to deal with fame all her life. When people meet her the first time, she knows that all they're thinking is, "Wow, I'm talking to Big Beef Broderick's daughter."

I took a deep breath. But before I could speak, Ti An interrupted. "We didn't do anything wrong, did we?" Ti An asked. "We've been trying to be so good."

54

"Yeah," said Jodi. "Good as spit."

"That's the problem," I said. "Thanks, Ti An and Jodi. You made it easier for me."

"Huh?" said Jodi. "I don't get it."

"I miss you kids," I said.

Cindi looked around. "We haven't gone anywhere. We've been right here."

"That's not what she means," said Darlene.

"You've all been avoiding me," I said, "walking around on tiptoe whenever I'm around, shushing each other. It's driving me nuts."

"It's driving *us* nuts, too," said Cindi. "I *hate* having to be so quiet. It doesn't go with my nature or my red hair."

"Oh, Cindi," teased Lauren, "redheads are even rarer than blondes — you'd better not go to Europe. You'd be mobbed."

"Cut it out," said Cindi. "Let Heidi talk."

"No," I said, "that's the point. I like it when you guys fool around. It's been kind of lonely lately. It's hard enough getting ready for the Olympics and feeling like everybody wants a piece of me. Then, when you all disappeared, I just hated it."

"We thought that was what you wanted," said Ti An. "Your mom said that you had to stay centered."

"The Pinecones are my center," I said. It sounded goopy and sentimental, but I really

55

meant it. I couldn't imagine having to be thousands of miles away at the Olympics without them. I would just have to find a way to make sure that they could come.

"That sounds like it belongs on a greeting card," said Jodi. Trust Jodi not to be taken in by my getting too schmaltzy.

"Well, it's true," I insisted. Dr. Joe had taught me that there were times when you shouldn't be afraid of getting mushy. "Anyhow, I need you. And if there's any way that we can swing it, I want *all* of you at the Olympics with me. I'll need a cheering section. You'd better all get passports."

"You're kidding," said Lauren.

"It's a proven fact that if the only one from this gym at the Olympics is Becky Dyson, I'll barf for sure," I said.

"Heidi Ferguson is not supposed to talk about barfing," teased Jodi. "The media will think the great Heidi Ferguson is up to her old tricks."

"Scandal! Scandal!" hooted Cindi. Cindi's got a loud laugh.

"What's Darlene's secret?" asked Ti An.

We all looked at Darlene. Darlene had a big grin on her face, as if she had swallowed a canary, although I've seen cats with birds in their mouths and they don't grin. It's a pretty stupid saying.

"Come on, Darlene, what's the secret?" I asked.

"Well, I didn't want to tell you because I was worried that you'd think I was like Becky."

"Yeah, you two are hard to tell apart," I teased.

"I'm going to the Olympics, too," said Darlene. Her voice sounded so excited.

"You are?" I exclaimed. "Why didn't you tell me?"

"I just found out last week, and it just didn't seem like the right time to make a big announcement. But my dad's been hired to do commentary for TV. He used to be a shot-putter in college, and he knows all the track-and-field stuff. He arranged it so that Mom and I could go, and the network rented a big apartment for us. It would be big enough for all of us, I think. I'd have to ask my parents."

"I can get tickets for the events," I said. "We've just got to figure out a way to get you all over there."

Cindi shook her head. "Count me out," she said. Cindi's dad's been out of work. He's an airline pilot, and he's been laid off. I know he's gotten part-time work at a desk job, but money's really tight in the Jockett family.

"Maybe you can put Cindi in your luggage, Darlene," suggested Lauren, "if you take a few less clothes." Darlene loves clothes, and she never travels anywhere without a huge suit-case.

"Forget it. It's first class or nothing," said Cindi sarcastically.

"Now there's an idea," I said.

"I was kidding, Heidi," said Cindi.

"No, the first-class tickets cost about triple what a regular flight costs," I said. "I've got a way to get all of you a free trip to Spain."

"Yeah, we can all start gluing feathers on our arms," said Jodi. "We'll flap our way over there."

"No," I said, "I've got a better way. I just have to work out the details."

"Heidi," said Darlene, "this isn't exactly the most important thing in the world that you should be spending your time on right now."

"Yes, it is," I argued. "You all thought I was kidding. But you *are* my center. Without you, I'd be nothing." I sang out the words, but I really meant them.

"Oh, golly," said Jodi. "Now she's singing songs. This is getting embarrassing."

"And she's got the worst voice west of the Rockies," said Lauren.

"East of the Rockies, too," said Cindi.

"Shut up, you guys. I tell you, this is going to work. I glanced up at the clock. Dimitri would be waiting for me.

Dimitri was tapping his foot impatiently. "All

right, little bug, ve vork again, right?" I knew he wasn't really mad at me. All month I had been having the best workouts of my life.

"Let me tell you my great idea." I told him my plan for bringing the Pinecones with me.

Dimitri listened to me. He stroked his moustache. "Ve bring Patrick, too," he said. "I could use an assistant."

I nodded.

"It's guud," said Dimitri. "The Pinecones vill help you have fun."

"They keep me centered," I said to Dimitri seriously.

Dimitri stared at me. "Centered — this I don't understand. What is this 'centered'?"

"Oh, it's just an American thing," I said. I didn't want to explain exactly what I meant to Dimitri. But I knew it was something that Dr. Joe would understand. "Are you sure you don't mind? It'll mean a sacrifice for you, too. You won't be able to fly first class."

Dimitri grinned at me. He's got an amazing grin. His whole face crinkles up. It's why I'm always willing to work so hard for him.

"For you — for the Pinecones — I put the cowboy boots in the luggage and these long legs go coach again."

I gave him a hug. "Thanks, Dimitri," I said. "Now I've just got to convince my mom."

10

My Dad Is
Hard to Figure

Mom wasn't at all happy when I announced my plan. "You what?" she exclaimed.

"I called the travel agent," I said. "It turns out that if you, Dad, Chris, Dimitri, and I trade in our first-class tickets to Barcelona, we could afford to bring all the Pinecones."

"That's ridiculous," said Mom. "You have to be joking."

"No joke," I said. "I want them there."

Mom turned to Dad. "Was this *your* idea?" she insisted.

Dad shook his head. "I did say to you that I thought it would be more fun for Heidi if some of her friends were there to cheer her on."

"You didn't tell me that," I said to Dad.

"I was going to talk to you about it," said Dad. "It slipped my mind."

"Dad, we leave for the Olympics in a few weeks! When were you going to get around to it?" I asked him.

"Anyhow," said Mom, "it's beside the point. Heidi, it's a silly idea. You will need your rest on the plane. I won't have you sitting in steerage."

"It's coach, Andrea, not steerage," said Dad.

"I think it's a neat idea," said Chris. "I'm willing to trade in my ticket."

"Me, too," said Dad so softly that I could barely hear him.

"The Pinecones can all stay with the Brodericks," I said. "It turns out that Big Beef is already going to do commentary on the shot put and track and field, so Darlene already has her ticket."

"I'm glad she finally told you," said Chris.

"You knew about it and you kept it a secret?"

"Darlene made me promise," said Chris. "She felt really awkward about it 'cause she knew the other Pinecones would be jealous. She was even thinking of not going if they couldn't go, but I told her that would be insane."

"Well," sniffed Mom, "I can see you think you've got this all figured out. But if you won't listen to me, at least you'll listen to Dimitri. He'll talk some sense into you."

"I already spoke with him," I said. "He thinks it's a good idea."

"With his long legs, he's willing to sit in coach so a bunch of silly girls can come along?" Mom asked, increduously.

"They're not silly girls," said Dad. "They're the Pinecones. They're her friends."

I was so relieved to hear Dad say that. "Thanks," I whispered to him.

He nodded to me.

Mom still looked very annoyed. "Marshall Marshak was going to fly over with us from New York to Spain," complained Mom. "He thought it would be a good chance to get to know you. *He* flies first class."

"You can fly up there with him," I said. "You can tell him all about me."

"That's not a bad idea, Andrea," said Dad. "We can afford it."

"Well," said Mom, a little bit more accepting of the idea now that she knew it wasn't *she* who was going to have to sacrifice her own comfort. "I think at least one of us should sit with Marshall."

"You, Mom!" Chris and I said together. Chris giggled. Dad frowned.

"That's enough, you two," he said. He got up. "I've got to get to work. Heidi, I'll have my secretary make those travel changes for you. I'll call the Brodericks and make sure that they don't mind acting as chaperons. You'll be in the Olympic Village, and we'll be a little too busy with you." Dad glanced at Mom. We both knew that Mom would have hated having to chaperon the Pinecones.

"Then you'd better check with all the Pinecones and make sure that it's all right with their parents if they come along," continued Dad. "Check that they all have passports. We can get them quickly if they don't. Tell their parents they can call me with questions. It's a lot to arrange in a short time."

This was my dad at his very best, taking care of details, taking charge.

"Thanks, Dad," I said. He grinned at me.

Mom was giving us a kind of dirty look. Dad gave me a very quick hug. "Just be sure you make all those phone calls," he said gruffly.

My dad is very hard to figure sometimes.

11

I Need a
Sports Psychologist

The Pinecones couldn't believe it when they found out that I had coach airplane tickets for everybody and passes for all the Olympic gymnastics events.

"It's a dream come true," said Cindi. She looked really grateful.

"I hear that Barcelona can be very warm in July and August," said Darlene. "And yet, it's supposed to be the most stylish city in almost all of Europe. I don't know what to wear."

"Just get Chris out of those nerdy short-sleeved shirts, will you?" I said.

"You're right," said Darlene. "He'll probably be on TV because he's your brother. I gotta straighten that guy out."

"I've got a guidebook for Barcelona," said Lauren. "It's a proven fact that it's supposed to be the most architecturally interesting city in all of Europe."

"Oh, no," moaned Jodi. "We're not going to spend all our time looking at monuments, are we?"

"Picasso grew up there," said Lauren, her nose in the guidebook. "He was a great artist when he was just a teenager."

I really wasn't interested in historical tidbits about Barcelona. I went to join Dimitri and Patrick. Dimitri was talking with his hands.

"You vill find it unbelievable," he said excitedly.

Patrick turned to me. "Dimitri got me an assistant coach's pass," he said. "I'll be able to go on the floor with you."

"That's terrific," I said, but I knew I didn't sound as enthusiastic as I should. I was thrilled that the Pinecones and Patrick were going to be able to come with me. I was proud of myself that I had been the one to make it happen, but I felt a little removed from it all.

I had a great workout. Working hard becomes a habit, a serious kind of fun. I get satisfaction from pushing myself to the limit in workouts, not just in competition. I know that all the effort, sweat, and pain pay off.

I had my last session with Dr. Joe after my workout. I wouldn't see him again until after the Olympics.

I got to his office a few minutes late because Dimitri had kept me overtime. Dimitri still didn't have confidence in my triple dismount off the uneven bars. He wanted me to practice a safer routine. We wouldn't decide until Barcelona whether I would do the triple or not.

Dr. Joe was saying good-bye to another patient when I got there. Sometimes I forget that Dr. Joe has other patients. This boy was an overweight kid about eleven years old. He looked very unhappy.

Dr. Joe signaled to me that it was okay to go into his office and sit down. I stared at the fish for a few minutes.

"Well, I did it," I said, trying to sound triumphant. I knew that Dr. Joe would be proud of me. "I talked to the Pinecones, and they aren't giving me the silent treatment anymore. Chris, Dad, and I are handing in our first-class tickets so all the Pinecones can go to Barcelona. It's all working out. My dad's been terrific."

Dr. Joe gave me a smile. "What about your mom?"

"She's going first-class because she has to talk to this agent she's hired for me."

Dr. Joe nodded.

"You think I need an agent?" I asked him.

"I don't know," he said. "It depends what you want to do after the Olympics."

"After the Olympics . . ." I muttered. I was feeling as if there were no life after the Olympics.

"Are you nervous?" Dr. Joe asked.

"Who wouldn't be?" I shouted, a little louder than I had intended. "Wouldn't you be?"

"What's the pressure like?"

I watched the fish swimming in and out of the castle. They didn't seem to care who was first, but the more I watched the more I realized that the same fish always led.

"If I lose, I'll always have to live with the fact that I went to the Olympics and failed."

"Every four years only six female gymnasts in the country ever go to the Olympics. That's not exactly failure."

"It's the way I'll look at it," I said. "Ever since I arranged for the Pinecones to come, it's as if I almost don't care. I don't mean about winning. I mean, about their coming. I wouldn't say that to anybody else but you."

"It's okay," said Dr. Joe. "Nobody but you or I ever knows what goes on in this room. The Pinecones aren't the ones feeling the strain. You are."

"I wouldn't be at the Olympics if it weren't for them," I said.

Dr. Joe raised one eyebrow.

"It's true. They keep me centered. That's what I told them."

"What does that mean?" Dr. Joe asked.

I stared at him. "Centered? Isn't that the kind of thing shrinks say all the time?"

"I don't," said Dr. Joe. "I'm not sure what 'centered' means in your case."

I sighed. "The Olympics, it's such a pressure cooker."

Dr. Joe didn't look sorry for me. I slunk down in my seat and played with the laces on my sneaker. "The pressure, the pressure." I kept repeating the word.

Dr. Joe coughed. He looked as if he was trying hard not to laugh.

"What!?" I demanded. "You don't believe that I'm under stress right now? What do you think made me sick in the first place?"

"Not gymnastics," said Dr. Joe matter-of-factly. He was making me mad. A shrink was supposed to be sympathetic to the pressure of the Olympics.

"You know, maybe Mom was right," I said spitefully. "She said that she thought I needed a sports psychologist, not just somebody that the hospital assigned to me. I'm not trying to insult you or anything."

"Right," said Dr. Joe.

Dr. Joe is like Patrick. He's almost never sarcastic. I looked up at him.

"You tell me," I said. "How do *you* think I should handle it?"

"The way you always handle this kind of pressure," he said. "It's the part of you I trust the most."

"What part is that? The part that makes me want to throw up after every meal?"

"Heidi," snapped Dr. Joe, "cut it out. I do not feel sorry for you because you're going to the Olympics."

"I wasn't trying to make you feel sorry for me," I whined. "Nobody knows what it's like."

"You tell me," said Dr. Joe. He waited.

My mind went blank. I couldn't think of what to say. "Nobody remembers that I have to compete."

"What got you into the Olympics in the first place?" he asked.

"I don't know," I shrugged.

"You like winning more than anything."

"That makes me sound so single-minded," I mumbled.

"I love that part of you that's so fierce about winning," said Dr. Joe.

"Yeah, so fierce that I tried to kill myself."

"Loving to win had nothing to do with your anorexia," he said. "The anorexia came about in some ways because you refused to admit how much you love to compete."

"I know that already," I snapped. "I hate it when you keep telling me things I already know. What you don't know is that it's Mom who hates to compete. The only way she knows how to do it is through me, and she always messes me up. And she's not me. Mom and I are different."

"Just different?"

"I don't know why we're going into this stuff right before the Olympics. It's the last thing I need to hear right now. This is really stupid."

"I don't think so," said Dr. Joe. "I think it's important."

"We should be talking about competition," I said. "You should be psyching me up. You know, Mom never really competes. She doesn't play any games, even tennis." I paused.

"Yes?" asked Dr. Joe.

"Nothing?"

"You were saying that your mother doesn't like to compete in games," said Dr. Joe. "I'd say that maybe she just doesn't like to compete, period."

"Mom doesn't compete and I do," I repeated softly.

"And?"

"I win. She doesn't," I whispered.

Dr. Joe nodded. "You're on to something, Heidi. It's sad, but it's not worth trying to kill

70

yourself over, and that's what you did when you stopped eating," said Dr. Joe.

"You are the one who keeps telling me it's not all her fault. Oh, I don't know why we're talking about this. It's really lousy. I don't think I needed to go into this junk right before the Olympics."

"This is as important as anything else we could talk about. No matter what happens at the Olympics, you'll still have to deal with this."

"Gosh, you really know how to cheer a person up."

"Heidi, I know it's painful, but remember, you *have* been dealing with it. You've been getting better and better." He grinned. "So much better, you're off to the Olympics."

I tried to smile back at him. I looked at the clock. We had gone over the time for my session. I stood up. I didn't feel very happy. Nothing seemed solved.

Dr. Joe gave me a hug. "Knock 'em dead at the Olympics," he said.

"You mean literally?" I teased. I stopped. I really didn't want to leave his office. "I'm sorry for what I said about a sports psychologist."

"Today, I was one," said Dr. Joe.

I looked at him as if he were crazy. I couldn't think of any sports psychologist talking about my mother instead of trying to motivate me.

"Good luck, Heidi," he said. "And remember

you can call me any time. I'll be here in September, after the Olympics."

"Are you going to watch?" I asked him.

He nodded. "Every minute that you're on," he promised.

Somehow that made me feel a little better.

12

The "Simple" Pinecones

The plane from Denver to New York left right on time. It was a good omen. Mom sat in first class with Dad, who had decided to fly first class after all. He said that he could get a free upgrade with all his frequent-flier miles.

That left poor Dimitri and Patrick in the back with me, Chris, and all the Pinecones. Patrick didn't seem to mind. He was in a great mood. Dimitri seemed preoccupied. So was I.

I sat in the middle between Lauren and Darlene. Cindi, Jodi, and Ti An were right behind me. Ashley was in seventh heaven because Becky had allowed her to sit next to her in a more forward part of the cabin. It had been just my luck that Becky happened to be on the same flight with us.

Lauren kept asking me if I wanted the window seat. I told her no.

We had one of those pilots who loves to give travelogues.

"If you look out the left-hand side, you'll see the Mississippi River," he announced.

"Big deal," I said.

"I love it when the pilots do that," said Lauren.

"My dad used to talk to the passengers," said Cindi. "He said that it was a pity for them to miss the geography."

"I hope our pilot points out sights from New York to Barcelona."

"What's he going to say?" I asked. "If you look down, you'll see more of the Atlantic Ocean?"

Lauren unfolded a big map that came in the back of the airline magazine. "We'll be going right over the Azores — they belong to Portugal. If we dipped down a little, we'd be taking practically the same route that Columbus took five hundred years ago. Did you know that New York City, Denver, and Barcelona are all on the same latitude? They're all much farther south than London. Most people don't know that. They think if you went straight from New York, you'd hit London, but that's not true."

"Let's hope you'd hit Spain," said Darlene.

"No, Portugal," said Lauren, studying her map.

"Geography is not my best subject," I admitted.

"It should be," said Lauren seriously. "Just think of it, you've been to Japan. You've probably been around the world. We should keep a map of all the places you've been."

"And I'm always seeing the same people and the same insides of gyms," I said.

"That's what my dad says about most of the football players he knows," said Darlene. "They never see the cities they visit. Dad does, though. He takes those guided bus tours in every city he travels to. He says he learns a lot from them, although the other Broncos think he's weird. He went to Barcelona a week early with my mom just so that they could have some vacation and really see the city."

"You won't need a bus tour," said Lauren. "You'll have me," she said. "I already figured out that the Olympic Village in Barcelona is down by the seaport, so we can pick you up from there and visit a huge Columbus monument. Columbus met the Queen of Spain in Barcelona. Then we can go up this great street called the *Ramblas*. They sell *everything* on that street: flowers and birds and chocolates, even monkeys."

75

"Any clothes?" asked Darlene who was sounding interested.

"Of course," said Lauren, still with her nose in her guidebook. "Barcelona is known for its style."

"I told you," said Darlene.

"I doubt if I'll be doing any sightseeing," I said, trying to stretch my legs. Maybe it was a mistake to have given up my first-class seat.

"I meant when you have a day off," said Lauren, sounding a little hurt. "I've been studying the schedule. You have the preliminary events the first three days of the Olympics, and then you've got a ten-day wait until the finals on the last weekend."

"Yeah, it's a schedule designed by somebody who likes to torture gymnasts. Whoever set it up that way should be shot," I grimaced. I really hated the schedule. I would die waiting.

Cindi popped over the back of my seat. "They did the schedule like that because gymnastics is the most popular sport for TV," she said. "They want to have it on the weekends so it can get the biggest ratings."

"Dad says that they think that over a billion people might be watching the gymnastics finals," said Darlene.

"Thanks, gang, you're helping me relax," I said sarcastically.

76

I was glad when the plane landed at Kennedy Airport in New York and we got to stretch our legs.

The plane seemed to take forever to empty out. I never get it. Everybody knows the plane is going to land. Why do people act surprised that it's time to get their coats on and get their luggage out of the overhead bins and get moving? It drives me nuts.

Finally, we made it out of the plane into the airport.

Mom was smiling, looking very cheerful and in a good mood. She and Dad had been able to get out right away. That's one advantage of flying first class, along with the leg room. Mom was talking to a tall man with snow-white hair and a deep tan. He looked like a millionaire cowboy.

Mom waved to me. "Who's that with your mom?" whispered Darlene. "He looks like a movie star."

"Got me," I said. "Probably somebody she met in first class. He certainly looks like he always travels first class."

"Heidi," called Mom, "see who was nice enough to come meet us at our gate. It's Marshall Marshak."

"Oh, goodie," I muttered under my breath.

"Who's Marshall Marshak?" whispered Lauren.

"It's a pretty dorky name," said Jodi.

"He's an agent," I said. I made a face. "Okay, gang, time to earn your keep. Don't let Mom get me alone with Marshall Marshak, okay?"

The Pinecones gathered around me, with no more questions asked. Mom frowned when she saw me coming with the gang.

She grabbed my shoulder and tried to pull me forward. "Marshall, this is Heidi," she said.

"I recognize you from your pictures and seeing you on TV," said Mr. Marshak. He had a funny squeaky voice that didn't go with his tall good looks. I guess maybe that's why he ended up being an agent instead of a TV star.

I shook his hand.

"And here is Heidi's coach," said Mom brightly. "Dimitri Vickorksoff, of course, you've heard of, and Patrick . . ." Mom paused as if she couldn't remember Patrick's name. I rolled my eyes up toward heaven.

"Patrick Harmon," said Patrick, stepping forward and shaking Marshall's hand. "I'm the owner of the Evergreen Gymnastics Academy where Heidi's been doing her training."

"And a very guud coach, the best," said Dimitri. I smiled at him. I had a feeling that Dimitri didn't like this Marshall character any better than I did.

"Well," said Mom brightly, "I think, Marshall,

maybe you and I should take Heidi somewhere where you can get to know her. We have a couple of hours between flights."

"And who are these other girls?" asked Marshall. "Are they on the American team? Alternates?"

Ti An giggled.

"Oh, no," said Mom, waving her hand in the air as if she were trying to swat away a swarm of pesky mosquitoes, "these are just the Pinecones, they're kind of like Heidi's fan club."

Cindi and Jodi glared at my mom. Those two definitely did not like to think of themselves as my "fan club."

"Mom," I scolded her, "the Pinecones are not a fan club. They're a team," I explained to Mr. Marshak. "They're my team. They made me an honorary member. I met them in the hospital when I was sick with anorexia." I knew Mom did not want me starting off my meeting with my agent by talking about my anorexia, but I didn't care. I wanted it out in the open.

"So you began competing with these girls," said Mr. Marshak. "That's nice. You must be one of the elite teams out of Denver."

Darlene made a snorting noise. "I don't think you've got it right. We're not elite. We're not in Heidi's class. We're just level six."

"They're a very good intermediate team," said

Patrick, defensively. "In fact, they're improving every day."

"Whatever," said Mom breezily. "Anyhow, Marshall, why don't you and Heidi and I go to the first-class lounge . . ."

"Wait a minute," said Mr. Marshak, "this is very interesting. Heidi, are you telling me that this simple group of average gymnasts were instrumental in your comeback?"

"They're the main reason I'm here at all, Mr. Marshak," I said proudly.

"Call me Marshall. We can do something with this. Girls, why don't I treat you all to a soft drink. Let's go where we can talk. Together."

"But, Marshall," protested Mom.

Mr. Marshak rubbed his hands together. "This is better than I even imagined," he said. "We can do wonders with this."

He led us all toward the lounge.

"Simple?" repeated Darlene as she and I walked together. She managed to raise one eyebrow.

"Average?" repeated Cindi.

"Darlene, wait till he finds out you're Big Beef Broderick's daughter," I teased her.

"Why, Heidi," gushed Darlene, "we were nothing before we met you. We Pinecones were put on earth just so that the sun would shine brighter for you. That's the kind of simple folks we are."

"Yeah," said Jodi. "Do you think he knows why a world-class gymnast is just like an elephant?"

"It sounds like one of Barking Barney's jokes." Barking Barney is Jodi's stepfather. He owns a chain of pet stores, and he always advertises on the radio with the stupid pet riddle of the week.

"It's not," said Jodi. "I just made it up. So do you know why you're just like an elephant?"

"No," I said.

"Because you've both got big heads," teased Jodi.

I groaned. I punched her on the forearm. "I don't have a big head. I wasn't the one who called you my fan club. Mom did."

"Only kidding," said Jodi.

I grinned. I was glad that the Pinecones were with me. I supposed that Marshall Marshak couldn't help his silly name, but I wouldn't have been able to stomach the Marshall Marshaks of the Olympic world without the Pinecones.

13

What's an Entourage?

When we arrived in Barcelona, the Pinecones went to the Brodericks' apartment. Mom and Dad took me to the Olympic Village and then went to the hotel. Barcelona is a port town, surrounded by green hills. The village was down by the seashore. The athletes who had been at other Olympics said that it was the most beautiful place to stay in the entire history of the modern Olympics. The Mediterranean Sea doesn't look at all like the Pacific or Atlantic Oceans. It looks much more like one of our Great Lakes, except the water is salty and very blue.

After a nap, I met my guide Melba Levick, who was a gymnast from Barcelona. Each athlete had been assigned a volunteer guide. Melba had light brown curly hair. She was fourteen, but she looked much older. She wore makeup, even early in the day.

Melba bragged that *La Villa Olimpica* was even more beautiful than anywhere the athletes could have stayed in Ancient Greece. It was brand-new. There were fanciful sculptures everywhere. The one that I liked the best was shaped like a giant fish. The dormitories, which would later become apartments, were painted red, yellow, and blue, the official colors of the Barcelona Olympics. It was very cheery, and clean. It was home to more than 15,000 athletes and coaches.

Nadia Malenovich was there. The great Russian gymnast makes Becky look like a pussycat. Nadia has the worst reputation among gymnasts. We all know that she will do anything within her power to win. She'll try to distract you on the floor, and that's just one of her ploys. She's been around a long time, and she knows all the tricks.

The rumor about the leading Chinese gymnast, Yang Li, is that the Chinese officials lied about her age, and she's really only thirteen. Chie Watsuta from Japan is probably my best friend on the international circuit. She's got a neat sense of humor. She's also an incredible technician.

Sonya Vlaidstock was there from Hungary. She

had trained with Dimitri until he had come to America, and she, like most of the Hungarian gymnasts, was not speaking to Dimitri. I could tell that it hurt him a little.

Dimitri was listed as the top American coach. It had been a battle to get him accepted, because some of the officials from the United States resented the fact that Dimitri had come over from Hungary and immediately got me to work for him. But it wasn't luck. The truth was that Dimitri is simply the best. I hoped that after this Olympics everybody would agree with me.

Dimitri told me he wanted me to keep up with my workouts twice a day, except on the days of actual competition. Most of the American team were not used to working as hard as I did, and they wouldn't be able to keep up with me.

The majority of the reporters and analysts were saying that the Americans had fielded the poorest team in years. With Chloe Chow out, I really was about the only hope for a medal. I'm not bragging — it's just that, except for me, there was nobody on our team who had scored in the top ten in *any* international competition. At least I had come in seventh in my last big competition in Japan. But that was when I was already secretly bulemic and not at full strength. Since I'd recovered, I had appeared in only one international challenge match, right in Denver.

I did really well in that, shaking up the competition.

Melba took me on a tour of the new Jordi sports arena where the competitions were going to be held. Lauren could tell you that it was designed by a famous Japanese architect. I only knew that the light in it was perfect. Light is incredibly important in gymnastics. Some stadiums have shadows in the weirdest places, and it can throw off your timing. Here, the entire stadium was bathed in uniform light. All the gymnasts agreed that it was the most beautiful indoor stadium any of us had ever seen. Even Nadia admitted that it was better than the one used in the Moscow Olympics in 1980.

"Oh," said Yang Li, "how did you do in the Olympics in Moscow?"

Nadia gave Yang Li a filthy look. "I was only eight years old, Yang Li. A little young, don't you think?"

Chie and I giggled. It was pretty funny to see Nadia and Yang Li with their claws out.

Unfortunately, we didn't practice in the Jordi sports arena. We had been assigned a practice gym, not too far from the *Villa Olimpica*. Dimitri and I had use of the equipment only from six in the morning until nine, and then again late in the afternoon.

The next morning, the Pinecones met me at

the gate to the Village to go to the practice gym with me. My parents were sleeping off jet lag at their hotel, but the Pinecones claimed to be too excited for jet lag. I had to agree with them. The time change didn't bother me. I was too thrilled to be here.

An Olympic mini-van drove us to the practice gym. I couldn't believe how many people were out at six in the morning.

"Does everybody in Barcelona go to work so early?" I asked Melba who was accompanying us.

Melba laughed. "They haven't gone to bed yet," she said. "Barcelona is the most sophisticated city in the world. We are famous for having the best night life in all of Europe. Madrid has nothing compared with us."

"I read that you don't go to dinner until nine or ten o'clock at night," said Lauren.

"Nine or ten!" I exclaimed. "I'm in bed by then."

"At the Olympic Village, they serve dinner all day long," said Melba, with a smile. "You can eat whenever you like." Her English was perfect. She spoke almost better than I did.

I looked out the window at the people. There were kids our age, laughing and walking arm in arm. Girls often walked with their arms around each other, as did boys. There were flowers for sale everywhere, and the light from the sunrise gave everything a soft yellow glow. I decided that I really liked Barcelona.

Then we got to our practice gym. The place was dusty as all get-out. It was an old gymnasium with no air-conditioning and really bad lighting.

"Hey," said Lauren, "we're right around the corner from the Gothic Cathedral. It's got a courtyard with real swans in it."

I sneezed. "I'm sure I'm allergic to swans," I snapped. "I've got no time for sightseeing."

I couldn't worry about Lauren's feelings. I was getting mighty antsy about how little practice time I had left. I was very careful with my warm-ups, taking the time to ease out any kinks that I might have from the long airplane ride.

Dimitri was standing by the uneven bars, testing them. "Are they okay?" I asked him anxiously, checking them myself.

"It's guud," said Dimitri adjusting the mats.

"So," I whispered to him, "let me try the triple this morning."

Dimitri shook his head. "No, not yet," he said. "Ve vant it to be a surprise. *If* ve use it. During the preliminary events, ve don't use it. You try it, and go splat — that's it. All America's chance for a medal goes *phhhttt*. You're the only American with a snowball's chance. Vithout you, zero — zip."

"Thanks, Dimitri, for keeping the pressure off," I grumbled.

"Listen, cookie, if you couldn't handle the pressure, you not belong here," said Dimitri. I knew he was right.

I looked around the gym and jiggled my shoulders to loosen them up. Gyms around the world are always the same. The beam is always four inches wide and four feet off the ground. The top uneven bar is always seven and a half feet, the lower one five feet. The vaulting horse is just one inch under four feet high.

It all feels like home.

"Beam first," said Dimitri.

I swung up onto the beam and took a few preliminary hops on it. It felt good. The beam had give to it. The gym might be dusty, but the Olympic committee had gone to the trouble of getting brand-new equipment even for the practice arenas.

My beam routine has a high degree of difficulty in it. That's to make up for the fact that I'm not the most graceful dancer of all time. The girls who love ballet always do better on beam than I do. Dimitri has designed a new move for me, called the Ferguson flair. It's fun because very few girls have the upper-body strength to do it. With all my weight on my hands, I hold myself above the beam and swing my legs on either side of the beam. It's similar to a move the men do on the pommel horse.

I practiced the Ferguson flair until my arms felt like overcooked spaghetti.

"Von more time!" said Dimitri.

"Von more time!" shouted the Pinecones from the sidelines.

I shook my head, but I laughed. Their being there gave me the energy to get back on the beam, and do it that one more time.

I saw Nadia and the Russian coach watching me. Beam is Nadia's best event. She deliberately walked in front of me as I was about to practice my dismount.

"Nadia, *oobeerat!*" Dimitri shouted at her in Russian.

Nadia just gave him a dirty look.

"What did you say?" I asked him.

"Move it!" said Dimitri.

I finished my routine with a back handspring to a full twisting layout. It's much tougher and more athletic than any landing that Nadia can do.

I landed with a thud, about two feet from where Nadia was standing, and I stuck it.

"Yes!" I shouted, and I pumped my fist at my side.

At the same moment, the Pinecones burst into cheers. I waved at them.

Nadia rolled her eyes. "I see you can't go any-where without those little girls to cheer you," said Nadia. "Part of your comeback, no? It helps to be like rock star with little cheepers always there."

"Nadia, those are my friends," I said, wiping off my sweat with a towel. "You met them in Denver."

"Yah, the Pinecones. From the fake native American tribe. You made it up to make fun of me." It was true that while she was in Denver the Pinecones had tried to convince Nadia that I was getting special "spiritual" assistance from a tribe called the Pinecones. It had been pretty funny.

"They are good kids," I said to Nadia. "Maybe four years from now they'll be here at the Olym-pics." I wanted to add that I would be back, too, but Nadia would probably be long retired.

"Fan chance," said Nadia.

"It's *fat* chance, Nadia," I said. "And they have a right to be here. They'll be good for me."

"Everybody talks that you are still fragile," Na-dia said to me. "I knew you needed those little kids before, but I told people Heidi Ferguson's better — she can stand on her own."

"Don't worry about my standing on my own," I said.

"Excuse me?" asked Nadia.

Nadia's English is perfect. She just has selective hearing.

"Never mind," I said.

I went up into the stands to sit with the Pinecones.

"What did Nadia Malenovich have to say?" Darlene asked.

"She thinks you're my entourage, like a rock star's."

"Oh, yeah?" said Jodi, who never backs away from a fight. "Look at *her*." We looked down on the floor. Nadia was surrounded by her dance coach, beam coach, personal masseuse, and hairdresser.

"What's an entourage?" asked Ti An.

"It's like we're Heidi's groupies."

"Is that a fish?" asked Ti An.

I laughed. The Pinecones were doing their job. They were making me laugh. I couldn't ask for more.

Dimitri was signaling to me and pointing to his watch. It was time to practice my vault. "The work never stops," I said. I handed my towel to Lauren.

"See, Ti An?" said Lauren. "This is what an

entourage does. We hold the sweaty towels for the great one."

The Pinecones kept me from getting a swelled head like Nadia. It all seemed so normal inside the practice gym. I was almost able to forget that in just a few days, a billion people would be watching me.

14

I Want the Gold

In the practice gym, it was easy to pretend that this was just another major international meet. Outside of the gym, the reality of the Olympics was everywhere. Marshall Marshak was always tracking me down, getting me to meet one corporate sponsor or another. Reporters from all over the world seemed to have heard of my struggle with anorexia and wanted to talk about my comeback.

I told Marshall that I wanted him to quit the hype, but he just shrugged and said it was too good a story. I hated being a "good story."

At least the reporters weren't allowed into the practice gym or the Village. I tried to stay focused and not get too caught up in all the Olympic hype.

But not all of the Olympics is hype. It was just incredible to be living with the top athletes of the world. When it was time for the official opening ceremonies, and I put on my sleek warm-up suit in red, white, and blue, I got goose bumps.

The opening and closing ceremonies were the only times that all the American athletes ever got together as a group. They were also the only times that we would all be dressed alike. Each of us had different uniforms for our specific events.

We gathered in one of the tunnels of the huge outdoor Olympic stadium. The stadium was located on Montjuïc, one of the beautiful hills overlooking the sea. Montjuïc was the site of most of the Olympic events.

The stadium was built in 1929, and it holds more than 60,000 spectators. It is just across the plaza from the Jordi Pavilion, where we would be performing our gymnastics.

The American athletes were all different sizes and races. If we weren't all dressed in red, white, and blue, there'd be no way to tell that we weren't African or Japanese or Scandinavian, German or Russian or Irish.

In the staging area, we could hardly hear each other because of the helicopters hovering over the stadium. When I saw all the flags from every nation in the world, I got a lump in my throat.

It wasn't like me at all. I'm not the sentimental kind, but there we all were: athletes from all over the world. There were nations so small I had hardly heard of them, and giant nations, and we were all together in one stadium.

The audience was as much a part of the ceremony as we were. They all had flash cards, and when we marched out the entire stadium turned into a collage of the Olympic rings: blue, gold, black, green, and red. I knew that somewhere in the audience my parents and the Pinecones were flashing their cards. I hoped for one moment Mom was forgetting herself and just enjoying the glory.

The Olympic Flame was lit, and the crowd roared. The sound bounced off the walls of the stadium, and it seemed to suck me along with it. I could imagine the cheers spreading like waves all across the globe, binding us all together. For that one moment, it was hard to believe that there could ever be wars, that young people like us would ever have to fight and die instead of just competing for glory.

And then in a burst of fireworks it was over. All the athletes were bused back to our Village. Everybody was chatting and laughing, but not me.

Tomorrow, the preliminary events begin. I had to do well in the early events if the U.S. was going to have any chance for a medal in women's gymnastics.

That night, as I tried to drop off to sleep inside the Olympic Village, I did what I always do before a major competition. I mentally go through each routine at least twice, every move, imagining everything done perfectly.

I knew that I could do my routines in my sleep. Dimitri had put me through the drill so many times that if you woke me up from a sound sleep and put me on the beam, I could perform.

Tonight, though, I couldn't sleep. I tried to tell myself, "You've done these routines a thousand times, it's just a matter of doing them one more time." But I knew that this time was different. Everybody always remembers the one who won the gold at the Olympics. That's the name that goes down in history. The others are forgotten. I wanted the gold.

15

Dummkopf!

I got up at five-thirty and walked around the Village. Dimitri was up, too. I saw him sitting on a bench staring out at the sea.

I went over to him. "Did you have trouble sleeping, too?" I asked him.

"It all starts today," he said. "This is for real."

I smiled at him. "Today, your English is good."

He nodded. "I think of all my other Olympics — vith my Sonya, my Hungarian girls. You could be the best."

"You really think I'm that good?" I asked him.

Dimitri nodded. I knew he wasn't just trying to pump me up. He believed it, and I did, too.

We watched the sun coming up above the

water. I could see Montjuïc and the stadium, all looking so quiet now with the helicopters and fireworks of last night gone.

"I *know* you're that guud," said Dimitri.

We stood up. It was time to get ready for the preliminary events. In the preliminary events, you perform by team with the weakest girl on each apparatus going first and the best one last. The first few provide a base to build scores on, setting the stage for the last ones who, at the Olympics, should be getting 9.9s and 10s.

Dimitri had convinced the other American coaches that I was the best candidate for the gold in the all-around, so they planted me last. There were nearly three hundred gymnasts competing. I knew that if I could stay within the top ten, I'd have a chance for a medal. The top thirty-six would all go on to the finals. In theory, any of the finalists had a chance for the medal. But I knew the way the judges' minds worked. I had to impress them today.

I couldn't eat much breakfast, but I didn't worry. I knew this wasn't anorexia coming back — it was just nerves. I could deal with a case of nerves on the first day of the Olympics.

I was as pumped up as I have ever been in my life. The Jordi Pavilion was packed as if this wasn't just the preliminary event but the finals.

The preliminary events can be tiring because so many gymnasts are competing. You have a lot of time to get cold between events.

Our first event was the vault. I was doing a Yurchenko layout full vault that had helped Mary Lou Retton win the gold medal. I flew into it with all my power and stuck my landing. I raised my fist in the air. I couldn't help it. I knew that vault was a 10! It was one of the best vaults I had done in my life.

Dimitri was jumping up and down on the sidelines. We waited for the judges' score. It was only a 9.8. The crowd booed.

"What did I do wrong?" I begged Dimitri.

"Nothing," he scowled. He glared at the judges as if he wanted to incinerate them. I felt awful. I couldn't imagine why I didn't get a higher score.

Then Chie Watsuta did the almost identical vault. She got a 9.78.

"Yah," said Dimitri.

"Yah?" I asked him.

"Forget scores," he said. "The judges. They going low. They vant to show they are tough!"

Dimitri turned out to be right. Even Nadia Malenovich got no 10s from the judges. I had often gotten 10s at meets, but I knew from history that it hadn't always been that way. Before Nadia Comaneci, almost nobody got a 10 in gymnastics. Apparently, the judges had decided to try to turn back the clock.

The commentators all talked about the low scoring in the preliminary events for this Olympics. It became one of the big stories.

I kept scoring in the low 9.8s — that's lower than I had scored in years, and yet in event after event, I found myself in the top dozen. I couldn't believe how well I was doing. I had only my bar exercise left. Nadia was on the beam, and she stumbled on her turn. I watched to see what the judges would do to her. If they scored her the way they were scoring the rest of us, she would have gotten a 9.4, but they gave her a 9.8.

I turned to Dimitri in a fury. "She gets the scores for who she is, not for what she does," I snapped as I put on my handgrips for my bar routine.

"So vat's new?" asked Dimitri. "You still ahead."

"I can sew it up if I do the triple," I said. "I've never been more on than today. I'm doing it."

Dimitri shook his head. "No, no!" he said adamantly.

I stamped my foot. I couldn't believe that I did something so childish. "Yes, yes! You've seen me today. I can't do anything wrong. I'm so hot, I'm burning. I can go into the finals so strong that they'll treat me like Nadia."

Dimitri shook his head. "This is just first day. Leave something to surprise them vith."

I was adamant. "If I do the triple, I break everybody. Nobody will catch me. It's just what the judges are waiting for."

"You do it and fail, and the judges think 'Ho, she's desperate.' "

I shook my head. I know my own body. Days like today are rare. Suddenly everything you've ever trained for comes together. Only an athlete can know this feeling, that exhilarating day when you are so in the groove, it's as if you can't fail.

"I'm doing it," I said to Dimitri.

The announcer called out my name on the loudspeaker. I saw the American flags waving in the stands. Everybody was counting on me to win a medal for my country.

I dipped my hands into the chalk bin and saluted the judges.

I took my position in front of the bars. My twist to the high bar was solid. I arched into a perfect handstand. As I swung up over the high bar, I reversed direction, letting go of the bar as I came over the top and catching it on the way down to the other side. It's a tricky skill that involves clearing the bar with both legs. I did it perfectly.

My giant swings were flawless. I heard the

crowd gasp as I let go of the bar and sailed high above the bars. I tucked into a tight ball, but I had too much power and momentum. I lost count of my turns. I hit the mats with my shoulder and bounced. Pain shot up my arm.

Dimitri gave me a filthy look. I knew I had blown it.

I saluted the judges, but I could barely raise my right arm. I didn't want to rub my shoulder, but it hurt like the dickens. I didn't want anybody to know I was hurt. My eyes welled up. It had happened so fast. I didn't believe it. I refused to believe it. I couldn't be hurt.

A photographer ran in front of me and stuck her camera in my face to get a close-up of my tears. I tried to squeeze my eyes shut to stop them, but I couldn't.

"Oh, please, not now," I begged. But all I could hear was the whirring noise of the photographers' automatic cameras. Finally Dimitri led me over to the medics.

"The score! Dimitri, what's my score!" I yelled at him. "I'm not hurt."

Dimitri looked back. "They gave you a 9.7, even with the fall. You vere perfect until then — dummy. I told you not to do that dismount — *dummkopf.*" Dimitri spat the words out at me. The fury in his voice shocked the medics.

I closed my eyes against the pain. I was a

dummkopf. I didn't know what I'd do if I was out of the Olympics. My shoulder still stung, and I couldn't lift it. The medics made me sit down in a wheelchair, and then they wheeled me into the on-site hospital. I had to be okay, I had to.

16

A Swarm of Locusts

"It's only a deep bruise," said the doctor for the American team. "No ligaments are torn. You're lucky. There's no permanent damage. You'll just have to rest it for a month."

"Lucky," I grunted to her. I winced as she moved the ice pack on my shoulder. She gave me an antiinflammatory pill. I didn't think much of her bedside manner.

"What do you mean a month?" I exclaimed.

"Four weeks — a month — you'll be fine."

I glared at her. "I've got ten days." I tried to move my shoulder.

"Don't," she said.

I ignored her. If it was only a deep bruise, I had

to keep blood moving in it, even if it hurt. Otherwise it would stiffen up.

"Get me the physical therapist!" I shouted. "And another doctor!"

My mother and father came rushing into the room. Mother was trailed by Marshall Marshak.

"Are you okay, honey?" asked Dad.

I adjusted the ice pack on my shoulder. "Just a bruise," I said. I tried to grin. Dimitri was sitting on a chair that was too small for him, with his hands dropped between his knees.

"What did you do to her?" Mom yelled at him. "How could she try a move in the Olympics that she hadn't prepared for?" Mom turned to Dimitri totally infuriated.

"Your *dummkopf* daughter almost did a quadruple somersault off the high bar."

I stared at him. "You're right," I said "That's what happened. I went around almost four times. Wow!"

"Wow is right," said Chris. "You were unbelievable. Are you hurt bad?"

"Naw," I said, trying to move my shoulder. I winced.

Another doctor came up and examined me. He was head of the American Olympic team. "You've got to tell me that I can come back for the finals," I said to him.

He examined the X rays that had been done earlier. He sighed. I didn't like the sound of his sigh.

"It's a very deep bruise."

"A deep bruise I can live with," I said. "Will I do permanent damage if I work out with it?"

"No," said the doctor. "But you'll be in too much pain to be full strength."

"Thanks," I said. "That's all I need to know."

"Wait a minute," he said. "We can't make any decisions until we see how the shoulder is. You'll have to see me tomorrow."

He checked the first doctor's prescription and told me where to go in the Olympic Village for an appointment with him and more physical therapy.

I stood up. The doctor helped me put the warm-up jacket around my shoulder. At least he was nicer than the first doctor. I walked over to Dimitri, who still looked so dejected. Patrick was standing by his side.

"Did I make it into the top ten?" I asked him.

"Yah," said Dimitri. "Then you ruined it all by going against my orders."

"Take it easy, Dimitri," said Patrick.

"No, I could wrangle her little neck," said Dimitri.

"That's strangle. Wrangle is what you do with your cowboy boots," I said.

"You'll see vhat I do with my cowboy boots!" shouted Dimitri. There was no mistaking the anger in Dimitri's voice. For a second I thought he might punch the wall.

Mom and Dad looked shocked, but I wasn't. When Dimitri's scared he gets furious. I had seen him that way before when I had hurt myself. I knew it would blow over.

"It's just a bruise," I said to him. "I thought the schedule was dumb because we had ten days off, but I can be okay in ten days."

Dimitri looked at the doctor, who said, "Well, I don't know about okay. Personally I doubt it. I know how much all you athletes want to believe you're superhuman, but none of you are. At least it's not the kind of injury that you can make worse by using the shoulder. Then I'd have to insist that you pull out of the games now. But I doubt if you'll regain enough motion in that arm to be able to perform at full strength. And anything you try will hurt you terribly."

"But you said it wouldn't cause permanent damage."

"No permanent damage, but there's a limit to how much pain one person can take."

"I don't care about the pain," I said. "I've got four years after the finals to rest."

"Are you saying she still has a chance?" asked Marshall. "Wait until the media hear the news."

I glared at him. "I don't want the media in-volved!" I said to him.

"Fat chance," said Chris.

I looked out the doorway of the clinic. There seemed to be about a thousand reporters lined up.

"I don't want to talk to them," I said.

"That's a mistake," said Marshall. "If we talk to them, we can control what they say. If you don't, they'll just write about you anyway."

"No!" I yelled at him. "I am not talking to any-body. Get it?"

"Heidi," snapped my mother.

"Let's everybody cool down," said Patrick. "Heidi's had a tough day. Let's get her out of here and back to the Village where she can rest. There'll be plenty of time to deal with the media later."

"Thanks," I said to Patrick.

I looked up and saw that the Pinecones had managed to wiggle their way up to the door of the clinic. I tried to wave to them with my left arm.

I heard the hum of the photographers' cameras grinding out picture after picture.

"Let's go," I said. Dimitri got on one side of me, Patrick on the other. Mom, Dad, and Chris walked behind.

"Heidi! Heidi!" screamed a woman whom I had never seen before. She stuck a microphone into my face and started babbling in French.

Dimitri tried to push her away. "*Alors — non comment!*" he snarled.

"Heidi Ferguson," said a very polite man with a British accent, "how badly are you hurt?"

"Are the Olympics over for you?" asked another reporter.

"Is it true that your anorexia contributed to your fall? Were your bones brittle?"

"My bones aren't brittle," I snapped.

"Shh," said Patrick, trying to push our way through the crowd. It was hard to breathe because the reporters pushed up against us. One of them shoved Dad, and he bumped my shoulder. I yelped in pain.

"Get out of the way!" yelled Dad.

"Obviously her family is very upset," said one of the TV commentators. "With Heidi today are some of the other anorexic girls from Denver, Colorado, her home town — they are Heidi's Ferguson's support team."

"Hey!" I heard Lauren shout. "We are not anorexic. We're Pinecones!"

And then finally, mercifully, the Olympic van showed up, and Dad and Patrick managed to get me into the front seat with Mom. Marshall, Dimitri, and Chris tumbled into the back.

Dimitri slammed the door to the van shut. I realized that we were leaving the Pinecones behind.

The reporters descended on them like a swarm of locusts.

17

The Spotlight

HEIDI HIDES IN PAIN

Heidi Ferguson, already weakened by her bouts with anorexia, took a terrible tumble.

The American star is listed as unlikely to be able to perform in the finals after her spectacular start.

"We won't let her quit," said Darlene Broderick, one of the lucky little gymnasts whom Ferguson has travel with her for good luck. Broderick is another recovering anorexic.

Experts say that Ferguson's anorexia and bulimia (anorexia is an eating disorder in which a person literally can starve herself to death — bulimia is a related disorder in which she forces herself to throw up all food) make it unlikely that she will be able to make the finals even if her shoulder heals.

The British tabloids were the worst. That article was from *The Daily Investigator*. They had made the whole thing up, but all the papers used the same tone. They all blamed my accident on my anorexia, and that had had nothing to do with it.

I threw the newspaper across the bed.

"Wow," said Jodi, "your shoulder must be okay if you can do that." I had just come back from the physical therapist, and the news was good about my shoulder. It hadn't stiffened up terribly overnight. Some of the newspapers, even the so-called respectable ones in the United States, were blowing the whole thing out of proportion. They had long articles on anorexia and bulimia, and showed pictures of me two years ago when I looked like a skeleton. I didn't look like that at all anymore.

"Where do they get off calling me another one

of your cheerleaders?" said Darlene. "And how did I end up being an anorexic?"

"You have been looking a little thin lately," teased Lauren.

"Why are they writing all that nonsense that I'm hurt because I'm anorexic," I protested. "It's a muscle bruise! It's got nothing to do with my anorexia."

"I'll never believe another newspaper story again," Cindi moaned.

"This newspaper got a picture of all of us getting on the plane," said Ashley. "I've got to fax that to my Mom."

There was a knock on the door. "Can you get it?" I asked Darlene.

Darlene opened the door. Nadia and Yang Li were standing there. "Oh," said Nadia, "I didn't realize you had company. We just came by to see how you were doing." She looked at all the newspapers that were piled high in my room.

"I'm doing better," I said, swinging my arm a little. "It's much less swollen."

"Do you think you're actually going to make the finals?" asked Yang Li. "The papers are saying that there's no hope."

"Don't believe everything you read," I said.

I got out of bed and stretched my arm. The physical therapist had agreed with me that the more I could make myself move it, the quicker it would heal.

Nadia picked up one of the papers. "Your picture is everywhere," she said.

"Yes," said Yang Li. "It's Heidi Ferguson this, Heidi Ferguson that. It's all anyone in the whole Olympic Village talks about."

"Whole Village? Try whole world," said Cindi. She picked up one of the Moscow papers. It had my picture on the front page. "Can you translate it for us, Nadia?"

"It's all — how you say — doggy-poo," said Nadia. "Heidi all the time, she does something to get herself in the paper."

"Hey," protested Jodi. "It's not Heidi's fault."

"Ha," said Nadia. "Two years ago when I was champion of the whole world — all they could talk about was Heidi Ferguson goes into hospital. Now, when I am about to win gold medal, you do it again."

"Nadia," I said. "I can't believe you think I wanted all this."

"Ho ho!" snorted Nadia. "You with that agent. And everybody knows Dimitri Vickerskoff is always trying to fool everybody. Don't try to act all innocent with me. You know you have no chance for the gold. It will be mine. Yet, you can't give up the spotlight. No, so you have all this nonsense."

114

Nadia kicked at the newspapers at her feet. She was furious. She really did believe that I had manipulated the press to get attention.

"I hate all this!" I protested. "I took a fall — that's all I did. I haven't done anything."

"Yah, yah," yelled Nadia. Her face was red. She was barely in control.

I stared at her. Here she was, champion of the world, and it wasn't enough for her. It would never be enough for her. Nadia would never be satisfied because the spotlight could never be bright enough for her. I couldn't lie and say that I wasn't a threat to her. I was. She couldn't stand the attention I was getting, and I couldn't stand the fact that she was world champion and I wasn't.

We really did hate each other. It wasn't a joke.

18

Clueless

I began working out the next day. It was hard because I was trying to compensate for the lack of strength in my shoulder by using my other side, and that threw me off balance. My beam routine was lousy. I kept falling off. I couldn't even think of doing the vault. I was too tender to get the power that I needed to get over the horse. But I could practice my floor exercise, and the simpler moves on the bars.

I had gotten used to *La Villa Olimpica*. When Dimitri asked me where I was going after a workout, I'd say home, and I meant the Village. I loved it as much as any place that I'd ever lived. Maybe more. I knew that all my life I'd remember my weeks at the Olympics, shoulder injury and all.

The air smelled salty from the sea. Whenever I walked on the beach, I could see the coastal patrol boats, making sure that terrorists or even just curious boaters never got too close. Maybe it was because of the tight security, but the Village was the place where I could totally relax. Reporters were not allowed to wander around unauthorized. They were allowed only in the press section. The rest of the Village was just for the privacy of us athletes.

I could walk around the Village and see kids from Argentina, Egypt, China, Kenya, hundreds of countries where they'd all been working just as long and hard as I had in the U.S. There was a lot of smiling and laughing, much more than the media ever caught.

All of us were on different schedules. The cafeteria, infirmary, and game rooms were open around the clock. Buses were coming and going twenty-four hours. Everywhere there were chain-link fences and security guards to protect us.

It was bright and sunny and homey. Everything was modern. Barcelona had surprised me by how modern it was. The clinic in the Olympic Village was one of the best I had ever been to. Unfortunately, I got to know it extremely well, and I got to know every other athlete who was hurting. There was a wrestler from Romania whose knee had completely blown up. But he was as determined as I was that he wasn't going to miss the Olympics.

In just five days, the physical therapy had improved the motion in my shoulder. Although I couldn't do nearly half of what I had been able to do, I was back to doing two workouts a day at the practice gym.

The publicity about me had died down, and I was thankful for that. There hadn't been any pictures or articles about me for days. I knew it would start up again when the finals began, but I was happy for the reprieve. As far as I was concerned, Nadia could have all the headlines. I just wanted the medal.

After the workouts, I tried to take Dimitri's advice, which was to go back to my room and rest. But I was getting very antsy with the wait. When my mom called and asked me for lunch, even an invitation from her sounded good.

"We'll just have a relaxing family meal," she said. I felt kind of bad that I had shut out my family since my injury, so I agreed.

I looked at my watch. I was late, and I was a person who was never late. When I got to the gate, I saw Mom pacing in front with Marshall

Marshak leaning against the gate, talking to reporters.

I muttered under my breath. Mom hadn't said anything about Marshall being there. I pulled down the Denver Broncos hat I was wearing so that it covered my face, and I wrapped my arms around my chest. I was wearing a Romanian satin wrestling jacket that I traded with my friend at the clinic for a Denver Broncos sweat-shirt that I got Big Beef to autograph especially for him.

"Heidi," said my mother, "I told you we were going to a nice restaurant."

"She looks fine," said Marshall. He saw the look on my face and shooed the reporters away.

"Just one second," said one reporter. "Heidi, can you tell us if it's true that your shoulder requires surgery?" I could tell from his accent that he was one of the British ones.

Luckily, Marshall had a cab waiting and we were able to jump in before I had to answer the stupid questions. The reporters seemed posi-tively disappointed that I hadn't ruined my gym-nastics career with my fall.

"I thought you wanted to have lunch with just the family," I said to Mom. I stared at Marshall. I didn't care if he knew I didn't want him there.

"Your father got a fax from the office," said

Mom. "He'll try to join us at the restaurant. Chris had a date with Darlene. They're going sightseeing with Lauren. I thought this would be a good chance for you and Marshall to get to know each other better without a crowd."

"No offense, Mr. Marshak," I said, "but shouldn't you be talking to Nadia Malenovich? She's the world champion, and she's got no intention of giving up the gold."

"She doesn't have what you have," said Marshall as he gave the taxi driver directions in fluent Spanish. I was impressed despite myself. I would have pegged him for the type of American who never learned another language, like Mom, Dad, and me, for example. This trip had made me realize what a dodo I felt like, speaking only English. Dimitri spoke four languages. The Romanian wrestler could speak Romanian, French, and English.

"What do I have that Nadia doesn't," I asked Marshall, "besides a sore shoulder?"

"Charisma, mystery, and spunk," said Marshall. "Nobody's exactly sure what's going on behind those dark eyes of yours. Everybody knows the Nadia type. She's like every movie star. Every move she makes is calculated. The press senses that you're different. That's why they've been after you this week."

"They'll forget about me soon enough, especially if I don't win a medal."

Marshall settled back against the seat of the taxicab. "Now that's where you're wrong," he said.

I didn't get it. The taxi pulled up in front of a restaurant near the *Ramblas*. Marshall paid and held the door open for my mother and me.

All the waiters were wearing tuxedos with big white aprons over their pants. There were huge mirrors on the wall.

"Picasso used to eat here," said Marshall. Then he said something to the waiter in what I thought was rapid Spanish. We were shown immediately to a big round table in the center of the room. I would rather have sat in a corner.

"Your Spanish is very good," I said to be polite.

"Oh, that was Catalán," said Marshall. "It's the official language of Barcelona. I know only a few words of it."

"Almost everybody I meet at the Village who isn't American speaks more than one language," I said. "When the Olympics are over, I am going to learn to speak Spanish. Maybe I can get Lauren's dad to give me private tutoring." Mr. Baca is a high school principal.

Mom looked very bored with that idea, but

Marshall seemed interested. "Lauren . . . is she one of the Pinecones?"

I nodded. At least he had gotten the team's name right — that was more than most of the reporters had done.

"I think there has been far too much about the Pinecones in the newspapers," said Mom. "After all, it's Heidi who's competing in the Olympics."

"Yes, but they're part of what makes Heidi so intriguing," said Marshall.

"Please don't talk about me like I'm not here," I sputtered. "What did you mean when you said it didn't matter whether I won a medal or not?"

The waiter handed us a giant menu. It was in two different languages, neither of them English. "You'd think with all the tourists they get here that they'd have a translation," said Mom.

"This isn't a place where tourists go," said Marshall.

Just then I saw somebody wave. I groaned. It was Becky.

"You're wrong," I said to Marshall. "It *is* where tourists go."

"Heidi," exclaimed Becky, "I'm so glad to see you! This is the restaurant that I wanted to take you to. I'm so glad you're getting out and eating." She gave me a kiss on both cheeks, as if she were European. "I've been leaving notes for you and messages, but I've been so busy, you've probably tried to call me and haven't gotten me."

"That's right," I lied.

"How are the Pinecones doing?" Becky asked. "I haven't seen them at track and field or the other events."

I didn't want to tell Becky that I had been able to get them access to the gymnastics practices.

"They're fine," I said. "Becky, this is Marshall Marshak — he's my agent. And I think you know my mother."

"How do you do?" said Marshall. He stood up politely. "I hope you'll excuse us, but I have business to discuss with Heidi and her mother."

I studied the menu and tried not to giggle, but I had to admit that Marshall was very efficient.

"How did you know I wanted to get rid of her?" I asked him after Becky went back to her table.

He winked at me. "That's my business," he said.

It was far too fancy a restaurant to be the kind that I really like, but Marshall Marshak was turning out not to be all bad.

He helped me order a rice dish with lots of different seafood in it, called *paella*. "It's their specialty," he said. Mom ordered the same thing.

Just then Dad came into the restaurant. He had a big smile on his face when he saw me.

"I like your Romanian jacket," said Dad.

I grinned at him. He shook hands with Marshall. "I'm sorry I'm late," he said. "So how's the shoulder feeling?"

Dad was the first one to ask me about my shoulder. "It's better," I said, moving it up and down a little. "I can do my floor routine almost full out. My beam is still lousy."

"I was about to tell Heidi," said Marshall, "that in terms of her marketability, this shoulder injury has turned out to be a godsend. You see, I meant what I said. It really doesn't matter whether you win or not. You're a human-interest story now. And you're young. Everybody knows that if you don't win a medal this time, you can do it four years from now. In fact, it almost heightens the interest if you *don't* get a medal."

I stared at him.

"Are you saying that Heidi should try to lose?" Dad asked incredulously.

"No, no," said Marshall. "I'm just telling you all that she doesn't have to sweat it. Everyone's taken with the fact that she's made a comeback from anorexia. I've had phone calls from producers interested in a TV movie. I've got three different cereal manufacturers interested in an endorsement. Here's a girl who used to be turned off on *all* food, and now she's big and strong on MuscleFlakes."

"MuscleFlakes? I don't eat those. They taste like cardboard."

"So we'll pick another cereal, or you can learn to like MuscleFlakes. This whole thing is dependent on the fact that your anorexia is cured. It could all blow up in our faces if you have a relapse. None of these sponsors is interested in an unhappy ending, but with a cure we don't need a medal. We've got our happy ending, and then we have the struggle to come back and win the Olympics four years from now. Of course, we'll have to put all the money in a trust fund so that you can keep your amateur status."

"I don't want to win the Olympics four years from now," I said. "I want to win now."

"Well, sure," said Marshall. "A medal would be nice icing on the cake. But I just wanted you to be able to relax."

"Icing on the cake!" I exploded. "You're nuts, you know that?" I said to him.

"Heidi," warned Mom, "don't talk to Marshall like that."

Marshall just chuckled.

"There's no reason to be rude, Heidi," said Dad. "I think what Marshall's saying is very heartening. He's telling you what we all want you to realize. It's fine if you don't win."

"It is *not* fine," I snapped.

"We just don't want you to put too much pressure on yourself. Remember that's what made you sick in the first place," said Dad.

125

"That's not what Dr. Joe says," I argued.

"Who's Dr. Joe?" asked Marshall Marshak.

"Dr. Joe List," said my mother. "He's one of the leading authorities on anorexia, although I'm not sure that Heidi wouldn't have been better off with a sports psychologist."

I shook my head. Mom was such a piece of work. "Dr. Joe is better for me than any sports psychologist could ever be," I said. I took a deep breath. I really wanted Mom and Dad to understand. "I want that medal. I want to win."

"No problem," said Marshall. "We all want the same thing."

Mom and Dad nodded, but I knew they didn't understand. I couldn't believe them. They hadn't heard a word that I was saying. We *didn't* all want the same thing.

Marshall leaned over. "You just have to learn to take things easy," he said.

I ate my *paella*. It was delicious, and I really was hungry.

Mom beamed at me as if being a media star was all that she wanted for me. Dad beamed at me because I was eating and that made him happy.

They didn't have the slightest idea of what I was about. Marshall sat back and seemed to think that everything was all hunky-dory.

They were all clueless. And I felt sad.

126

19

Be a Kid

The lunch with Mom and Dad had depressed me more than my shoulder injury. I was still in a bad mood the next morning, and I was mad at myself for feeling blue. I had only two days left before the finals. This was the time when I should be the most concentrated, the most focused.

I took the bus to the practice gym, barely bothering to look out the window at all the people.

When I got to the gym, Dimitri immediately noticed something was wrong. "The shoulder, it hurts?" he asked.

I shook my head. "No, it's better."

Patrick looked at me funny. He knew also that

something was hurting me and it wasn't my shoulder.

"Why the long face?" Patrick asked.

"Nothing," I lied. "Just got up on the wrong side of the bed."

"The vaiting — it's hard," said Dimitri. "But guud. The shoulder heals. Go varm up."

I took particular care with my warm-ups, because I knew from experience that when I was depressed I sometimes hurt myself.

Whenever I stretched my shoulder, I felt twinges, but I didn't wince with pain the way I had before.

I swung my arms in a swimming motion, able to do a full rotation.

I heard a cheer from the back. I looked up. The Pinecones were sitting in the bleachers.

I waved to them with my right arm.

"They cheer you just for a wave?" asked Nadia who had come in to begin her warm-ups. She was scheduled for the equipment right after me.

"They're cheering me because my shoulder's better," I told her.

Nadia looked worried. Good, I thought to myself. I didn't mind that Nadia worried.

I trotted over to Dimitri and Patrick. "Better?" Patrick asked me.

"Yes," I said. My mood had brightened now that I was in the gym. Or maybe just because the

Pinecones were there, and Mom was nowhere in sight.

"I'm ready to work the bars today," I said.

"Guud," said Dimitri, "but no triples."

He wasn't going to get any disagreement from me. As soon as I started swinging, I knew the muscle pain was not going to go away. But it wasn't unbearable.

Neither Dimitri nor Patrick treated me with kid gloves because of the injury. Dimitri had Patrick do the spotting so that he could watch me more closely. After my first pass at my routine, Dimitri was shouting at me, "No, no . . . terrible . . . terrible. The toes — they're not pointed."

"Relax," I said. "Aren't you happy that I can do it at all?"

Dimitri stared at me. "No," he growled. "Vot that mean, 'Relax'?"

I swallowed hard. With Dimitri there was no holding back. His philosophy was that you worked harder than any other gymnast in the world because you knew that there was no easy way.

"I'll do it again," I said.

"You're darn tooting," said Dimitri. I rolled my eyes. There is nothing worse than Dimitri when he tries to sound western.

But I did the routine again. Sweat was pouring

off me. When it was Nadia's turn on the bars, I switched to the vault. My shoulder was feeling a lot better, but Dimitri didn't want me to go full-out on my vault. He didn't want to take any chances. When Nadia came to the vault, I went up on the beam. She finished her workout after ninety minutes, and Dimitri still had me practicing my floor exercises. Finally, after two and a half hours, he signaled me that it was time to quit.

I felt good — exhausted, but good. My mood had changed. My legs were so heavy, I felt as if my knees were scraping the ground, but I knew that I was getting back to full strength. Soon I'd be as strong as any girl competing against me. I just hoped it would be soon enough.

The Pinecones came off the bleachers to meet me. I couldn't believe that they had stayed to watch the whole workout.

"You kids are gluttons for punishment," I said to them. "That must have been boring as all get-out."

Cindi's eyes were bright. "I loved it," she said. "You were hot."

I looked at them. I had forgotten what a tough competitor Cindi was. She understood me, and I could tell from the look in her eyes that Cindi had been bitten by the Olympic bug. She was only eleven. If she really got serious, being a contender wasn't beyond her. It really wasn't beyond any of them.

"What are you all going to do now?" I asked as I toweled myself off.

"We're going up to this great park," said Lauren. "It's called the Park Güell. It's by the architect Gaudi who does all this weird stuff."

"Lauren's been reading her guidebook again," said Jodi.

"Yesterday, we walked around the Gothic area," said Ti An. "It's got all these narrow streets, just like they had in the Middle Ages."

"It *is* from the Middle Ages," said Lauren. "This isn't Disney World. It's the real thing."

I laughed. "So far, all I've seen of Barcelona is the road from the Village to the practice gym and the bus up to Montjuic. And one fancy restaurant with my parents and Marshall Marshak." I made a face. "Becky was there."

"Was the food lousy?" Lauren asked.

"Actually, it was good. I had *paella*."

"That's got squid in it," said Ti An. I blinked. I was glad I hadn't known that while I was eating.

"Why don't you come with us?" Lauren asked.

I shook my head. "I've got to go back to the Village and rest," I said.

Patrick overheard me. "Why not take a break?" he said. "Go with the gang. It'll do you good to see a little of Barcelona."

"Dimitri might not think so," I said.

"Vot Dimitri think?" asked Dimitri. He came up to me after he finished talking to the Japanese coaches. Dimitri loves to talk to the other coaches.

"I think that Heidi should take a break today," said Patrick. "She's had a tough workout. We've still got two days before the final. Let her skip the afternoon workout and go out with the Pinecones."

Dimitri started to say no, but then he must have seen something in my face, because he changed his mind.

"Guud idea," he said. "Go have fun. But no reporters."

Lauren was excited. "Don't worry," she said. "The reporters all hang around the same places — the practice gym and the Olympic arenas. They'll never go to this park."

"Guud," said Dimitri. "Go be a kid."

Patrick nodded.

That's why I like my coaches.

20

Front and Center

"What is this place?" I asked Lauren. We were on top of a hill, overlooking Barcelona. The hill was covered with huge twisted pine trees. There weren't many people around. A giant lizard, made out of tiny chips of colored glass — orange, white, blue, and green — guarded the entrance to the park with its mouth open in a wide grin.

"This is Park Güell," said Lauren, looking up from her guidebook.

"That's some lizard," said Jodi, patting his back while Cindi took her picture.

"Come up here, Heidi!" shouted Jodi. "Let's get a picture together. Darlene, will you take it?"

Cindi handed Darlene her camera. "Heidi, take

off those stupid dark glasses, will you? I can't see your face."

"I don't want anyone to recognize me," I hissed.

Jodi grabbed my Broncos hat. "You've got a bad case of nerves," she said. "Look around. The park's half empty."

I climbed onto the lizard. Jodi was right. I was acting like a paranoid movie star. I stuffed my glasses and hat into my knapsack. "Okay, here's a headline for you: 'Heidi Ferguson rides a lizard,' " I said, spreading my arms out wide.

Darlene snapped our picture.

"It's not a lizard. It's a dragon," said Lauren. "It was going to be the entrance to a garden city by that guy Gaudi. He's the one who made the neat cathedral that looks like a drip sand castle over there."

Lauren pointed to six fantastical towers on a church not too far away.

"This place is neat," I said. I jumped up onto a wavy bench made out of the same brightly colored glass tiles. The glass twinkled in the sunlight.

"And now, the great Heidi Ferguson will attempt the bench walk," said Jodi, pretending to have a microphone in her hand.

"Shh," I warned her. "I don't want anybody to know I'm here."

Jodi plopped down on the bench. "So what's it like being rich and famous?"

"She was rich before," Darlene pointed out. I laughed. The Pinecones really did not take this rich and famous stuff at all seriously. I felt happy for the first time since I hurt my shoulder.

"I'm glad you guys are here," I said.

"And we're glad we can be here for you," gushed Jodi.

"Yes," simpered Lauren, "we Pinecones live and breathe for your happiness."

"Cut that out," I said. I picked up a real pinecone and threw it at her. "Pinecones to the Pinecones," I said.

"Uh, oh, pinecone fight, pinecone fight!" shrieked Ti An. She started gathering pinecones and pelting me with them. Darlene got ammunition, too. Soon all of them ganged up on me. "Nuts to the nuts," shouted Cindi.

"Stop, stop," I begged, laughing so hard I couldn't stop.

"That's what happens when you become famous," said Cindi, laughing. "People throw pinecones at you."

"Well, I don't like being famous," I said seriously. "It's a drag."

"Oh, yeah," said Jodi. "Tell me you don't like the fact that Nadia Malenovich is going crazy with jealousy."

"That part I don't mind," I admitted. I sat down on one of the benches and stretched out my legs in the sun. It was the first time in weeks, it seemed, that I had enough room to stretch out.

"It really is a drag having everybody misquoting you all the time."

"Tell me about it," said Darlene. "The tabloids are always writing that my mom and dad are getting divorced and all that gunk."

"I am *sick* of reading about my miraculous recovery from anorexia."

"So are we," said Ti An.

"Let's keep going," said Lauren. "There's more park above us. Then we can take a cable car to an amusement park called Tibidabo."

"I like that name 'Tibidado'," I said. It kind of tripped off my tongue.

"Tiba*b*o," Lauren corrected me.

"Tibidabo," I repeated. "Hey, when we get back, do you think you can try to tutor me in Spanish?"

"Why?" teased Lauren. "Did they ask you to endorse one of those sneaker ads in Spanish?"

"No," I groaned. "Don't talk to me about endorsements. That guy Marshall Marshak is talking about my doing a MuscleFlakes endorsement."

Jodie put a finger in her mouth and pretended to gag.

"You're right," I said, and I copied Jodi's gesture.

Just then I heard a whirring noise and a click.

"What the . . .?" I exclaimed.

From behind a tree, I saw someone dressed in camouflage pants and a jacket.

"Hey, you!" I shouted, waving my hands in his face.

Quickly the photographer stuffed his camera into his bag and took off down the path.

"Stop him!" I shouted. Lauren was the closest to him. She's a powerful runner. She's the fastest of the Pinecones. She just took off, but the guy had a taxi cab waiting at the entrance to the park. Before Lauren could catch him, he jumped in the cab and took off.

"Darn it!" I screamed. "Why couldn't he leave me alone?"

"You're getting too sensitive," said Darlene. "So he took a few pictures of you fooling around with your friends. You've got to stay cool. That's what my dad does."

"You're right, I guess," I admitted.

"Yeah," said Ashley. "They haven't shown a picture of you all week. Maybe I'll get in this one. Mom said that she could barely make me out in the one that I sent her."

"Oh, good, Ashley," I said. "I'll be sure to ask them to put you front and center."

"Could you?" asked Ashley.

I just closed my eyes.

"Heidi?" asked Darlene. "Will you stop acting like it's some kind of tragedy. After all, what would you have done if we had caught the jerk?"

I shrugged. "I don't know," I admitted.

"Then stop making such a big deal out of every idiot who wants to take your picture," said Darlene.

"Hey," said Cindi, pointing her camera at me. "I'm taking her picture. I'm not an idiot."

I gave Cindi a big smile. The Pinecones were right. I was taking everything too seriously. It was time to let loose and have fun.

21

No Statement

I had a great afternoon with the Pinecones. I slept better that night than any night since we had arrived. I woke up feeling terrific. I knew from experience that a good night's sleep was an excellent omen two nights before a major competition. There was nothing more major than the Olympics.

I stretched. My shoulder felt good. I went to the bathroom and had just started to brush my teeth when I heard a pounding on my door.

I rolled my eyes. "One minute!" I shouted.

The pounding got louder. Maybe whoever it was didn't speak English. It was probably Nadia wanting to borrow something.

I tried to put on my Miss Piggy slippers. One

of them was under my bed. "Hold your horses!" I yelled as the pounding continued.

I flung open the door, with my slipper in my hand, expecting to see Nadia or Chie or one of the other kids from my floor. Instead my mother was there.

"What the . . . ?" I exclaimed. My mouth was still full of toothpaste.

"Look at this!" shrieked my mother. She waved a newspaper in my face.

"Mom?" I asked. "What are you doing here?"

"Everything we worked for ruined. Oh, Heidi, how could you?"

"How could I what?" I asked. I didn't have the foggiest idea what she was talking about.

I took the newspaper Mom was shoving at me. I did a double take. "Unreal," I said, sinking back on my bed. I started to laugh. I couldn't help it.

Mom glared at me.

"What are you laughing at?" she demanded.

"This," I said, giggling. I looked again. Naturally, it was my old friend *The Investigator*.

HEIDI'S TRAGIC RELAPSE

The print must have been six inches large. They didn't even bother with my last name anymore.

Then right below the headline was a picture of me with my finger in my mouth, pretending

140

to gag. In only slightly smaller print were the words: *Olympic Star Has Relapse With Dread Eating Disorder.*

"Mom," I said, handing her back the paper, "it's not true. I haven't had a relapse. The stupid photographer caught me clowning around with the Pinecones."

"The Pinecones," snapped Mom. "I should have known."

I just grinned. "Anyhow," I said, "forget about it. Sorry it got you so upset, but I'm fine."

"Fine!" squawked Mom. "You call it fine! Young lady, don't you realize what this means?"

"Yeah," I said. "Some idiot is trying to sell newspapers with a stupid picture." I glanced at the photograph again. I looked pretty weird. "Wait till the Pinecones see this," I said.

"Heidi," said Mom, "I don't think you realize how serious this is. Marshall and your father are waiting for us down in one of the conference rooms. This is not a joke."

"Why?"

"Just get dressed," snapped Mom. She paced around my little room until I was ready.

In the communications center of the Olympic Village, there were several conference rooms with fax machines and telephones.

I was surprised to see that Chris was there, too. "Hi, sis," he said. "I liked your picture."

At least he was acting normal. "Everybody relax," I announced. "I haven't had a relapse. It was just a gag."

"Good choice of words," said Chris.

I laughed.

"I'm going to sue the paper," said Dad, furiously. "I knew it was all an outrageous lie."

"That won't do any good," said Marshall. "It'll only call attention to the whole issue. We've got to find some way to counterattack."

"Nobody reads *The Investigator*. I don't think it's even published in the United States," said Chris.

"It's in every supermarket," said Marshall.

"We've heard that the networks have picked up the photo and are using it on a special report about Heidi," said Dad.

"It's extremely unfortunate," said Marshall. "The sponsors who were interested in you are very worried. I've already gotten phone calls with second thoughts."

"Who cares?" I said.

Everybody ignored me.

"There must be an expert that we can get to testify that she's not anorexic. What about the doctor who's been treating your shoulder?" Marshall asked me.

"She's an orthopedist," I said.

"What about the doctor who treats you in Denver? Didn't you say he was one of the leading authorities on anorexia?"

"Dr. Joe!" exclaimed my mother with more warmth than I had ever heard her use toward him. "That's the ticket."

"Hold it, everybody!" I yelled. I was getting more than a little ticked off. "Forget the dumb endorsements. You don't need to call Dr. Joe."

"Heidi," said Marshall, "this is major."

My father nodded.

"You're all insane," I said. "It's one day before the finals of the Olympics. The one time you show up in the Village is to talk to me about this junk!"

"Heidi," said my mother, "Dr. Joe can help."

"You never wanted his help before," I said.

"Don't be childish," said my mother. My dad just looked on helplessly.

"We can hammer out a statement right now," said Marshall. "I'll get him on the speaker phone. What's his name again?"

"Dr. Joe List," said Dad.

"Do you have his number?" Marshall looked up at me.

I glared at him.

"Heidi," snapped my mother, "you must know his number by heart. I've got it in my book somewhere." Mother thumbed through her book and gave Marshall Dr. Joe's number.

I tried to remember what the time difference was, but I always get it confused.

Dr. Joe's machine came on the speaker phone. It sounded as if he were at the bottom of the ocean. I was glad he wasn't in. It served them all right.

"Dr. List, this is Marshall Marshak. I'm with Heidi Ferguson, one of your patients. We've got a little problem."

Dr. Joe picked up his phone. "Is Heidi all right?" he asked anxiously.

"I'm fine," I spoke up into the phone.

"Heidi?" asked Dr. Joe. "What's going on there? It's late at night. I just happened to be at the office, doing some paperwork. Where are you? What happened? Your shoulder?"

"My shoulder's fine," I said through gritted teeth.

Marshall interrupted. He explained about the photograph. "I don't know if you've seen some of the press reports about Heidi. They're talking about her anorexia."

"Who are you?" insisted Dr. Joe.

"I've been hired as Heidi's agent. Even if she doesn't do well tomorrow, if we can nip this crisis in the bud, she'll be fine. And there's always the next Olympics. We just need a statement from you that Heidi's cured. Sorry to make this so rushed, but if you'll just dictate it to me, I'll spruce it up and get it out to the press within the hour."

"I'll do no such thing," said Dr. Joe.

I clapped my hands. "Yea!" I shouted. "I told them they were nuts."

I could hear Dr. Joe laugh. "Heidi, let me talk to you alone."

"Look, Dr. List," intruded Mom, "all we need from you is one little statement saying that Heidi's over her anorexia. That's not so much to ask."

"I don't know who's listening in that room," snapped Dr. Joe. "But first of all, we never talk about 'cure' with anorexia. It's a little like alcoholism. Recovering anorexics have to learn to live with their problem and their attitude. Second of all, I would never, I repeat *never*, talk about Heidi to *anybody*. Is that clear?"

I had never heard him sound so angry.

"But what if we give you permission to issue this statement?" said my father.

"Even if Heidi herself asked me to make a statement, I doubt if I would. Heidi, do you want me to participate in this charade?"

"Are you kidding?" I said.

"Mr. Marshall, are you still there?" asked Dr. Joe.

"It's Marshall Marshak," said Marshall. "And I think you're being unreasonable."

"What you've asked me to do is completely un-professional. Now get me off that damned speaker phone and put Heidi on privately."

Marshall switched off the button for the speaker phone and handed it to me.

"Sorry," I said to him.

"It's not your fault," said Dr. Joe. His voice sounded normal now. It was an amazingly clear connection. He could have been just across town instead of across the ocean and a continent.

"So," he said. "You're not buying that non-sense about 'there's always another Olympics,' are you?"

"I'm here to win this one," I said.

"Good," said Dr. Joe. "Is your shoulder really okay?"

"Yes," I said. Dr. Joe sure knew what was important.

"If your shoulder's okay, I want you to win tomorrow."

"I will," I promised him.

"Good," said Dr. Joe. "I'll be watching. Good luck."

I hung up the phone.

"Well, he was certainly less than helpful," said my mother.

"You couldn't be more wrong," I said to her. "I'm getting out of here."

"Where are you going?" asked Marshall.

146

"I'm going to the gym," I said. "I've got one last practice scheduled."

"We still haven't resolved how to deal with this picture," stammered Marshall. He waved *The Investigator* in the air.

"You deal with it," I snapped. "Isn't that why Mom is paying you? That's your job!"

"But . . . but . . . we've got to put out some kind of statement," argued Marshall.

"I'll make my statement tomorrow," I said, "in the finals."

Chris gave me a thumbs-up gesture. Dad nodded. Maybe, just maybe, he was beginning to understand.

22

Sticks and Stones

The Pinecones were waiting for me in the gym. They looked very subdued.

"Are you okay?" asked Patrick.

"You saw that picture," I said flatly.

"We all did," said Darlene.

"I would have made him eat his camera," moaned Jodi.

"It's all my fault," said Cindi. "I was the one who started fooling around.

"No, I was," said Darlene. "I started teasing Heidi about her dark glasses. I'm to blame."

"I wanted to be front and center," said Ashley.

"It was my idea to go sightseeing in the first place," groaned Lauren.

"If I find that guy, I vill take his camera, and

it goes down his throat," said Dimitri fiercely.

I put my hands over my ears. "Stop!" I shouted. "It's nobody's fault, and it's not that big a deal." I looked around at the Pinecones. "Don't you start acting like my parents." It was the greatest threat I could make.

Darlene pretended to button her lips. "Good," I said. I pointed to the bleachers. "Go, I've got a workout to do."

Dimitri raised his eyebrow. "Ve vork," he said.

"Yes," I answered. "Ve vork." I was still angry about the way my parents had reacted to the photograph, but I made myself calm down. I breathed into my stretches. I knew that the anger would just get in my way. You can't think if you're too excited, and in gymnastics you need to be thinking all the time.

I finished my warm-ups and went over to Dimitri. "Let me practice on bars again," I said to him. "The other routines are fine."

Dimitri shook his head. "No, no. We go through each one. Method. Method."

I looked into Dimitri's eyes. He looked as determined as I did. Neither of us mentioned the photograph or the press. This was where he and I belonged. We had one of the hardest workouts ever. My shoulder still bothered me on my vault and on the beam, and even on the floor exercise, but I ignored it. Dimitri picked apart every move that I made and had me do it over and over.

I really worked up a sweat, and the more I sweat the more concentrated I felt.

Finally we moved over to the bars. The gym was still extremely quiet. The Pinecones were the only spectators, and they sat in the bleachers as if they were in church.

I grabbed the lower bar and started swinging. The feeling of flying free is what I've always loved about the bars.

I beat against the lower bar for greater momentum. That rhythm has always come naturally to me. At the height of my giant swing, I let go and tucked myself into a tight ball. I revolved around myself, a spinning top, but this time I kept the count, kept track of where I was in relation to the floor. Everything seemed slowed down as if I had all the time in the world. I straightened out my legs and hit the mats. The force with which I landed caused me to fall to my knees. I hadn't stuck the landing, but I had done the triple. I rubbed my shoulder. It had begun to ache.

"Guud," said Dimitri. "But your feet too far forward when you land. Enough. Ve save something for tomorrow."

He handed me a towel to wipe off my sweat. Nadia had entered the gym. I knew she had seen me on the bars — I could tell from the worried look on her face. She began to chalk up.

"Where are they?" she asked me.

"Who?" I asked. "My friends are in the bleachers." I pointed to the Pinecones.

"That's not who I meant," said Nadia with a sneer in her voice. "The photographers. I thought you didn't do anything without them around."

"They'll be there tomorrow, Nadia," I said. "Tomorrow they can take all the photographs they want."

"Tomorrow, they will be interested only in me," she said. "Tomorrow it is gymnastics that counts — nothing else."

"That's how I want it," I said.

"Tomorrow I take home the gold medal," she said. "No more second fiddle to sob stories about Heidi Ferguson."

"It won't be sob stories about Heidi Ferguson that you'll be reading," I told her.

Nadia turned her back on me. I wiped the sweat off my body. The words came easy. The old rhyme came back to me. "Sticks and stones can break my bones, but words can never hurt me." Tomorrow, Nadia and I would go at it with more than words. Tomorrow was the day for sticks and stones.

23

Try Not to Fall

Usually before a major competition my dreams are very up. I see myself doing everything perfectly, but that night, I had a nightmare. I was on the bars, and I just kept going around and around and around, and it wouldn't end. I sat up in a sweat.

I don't think that I slept more than forty-five minutes all night.

I had heard other athletes in the Village say that you had to treat the Olympics as just another competition. They tried to tell themselves the fact that the whole world was watching didn't matter. I couldn't. I was so pumped up after my nightmare that I didn't even try to go back to sleep. At dawn I took a walk around the Village. It had begun to empty out. The finals for the gymnastics medal was the last event before the closing ceremonies.

The Gymnastics All-Around had become the hottest ticket at the Olympic games. Everyone was expecting that it would all come down to Nadia and me. It didn't matter that the cold war was over. She was Russia. I was the United States. Each of us was expected to win for our nation's pride.

The finals were not scheduled until late at night, so that the event could be televised live during prime time in the United States. It was the worst time in the world for me, but there was nothing I could do about it.

I stayed by myself in the Village all day. I didn't want to talk to anybody. Finally, it was time to board the vans to the Jordi Pavilion on Montjuïc. I knew that every one of the 17,000 seats in the Pavilion was sold out. The crowds had already started to gather, even though the first fanfare wouldn't begin for hours.

Everything was brand-new at the Jordi Pavilion. We finalists were herded into the multipurpose annex that was fully equipped with practice equipment. We would be able to do our warmups without having to go into the main arena.

It gave us a final moment of privacy. Only spectators with special passes were allowed into the annex.

I could feel the tension. There was no chatting between gymnasts today. No one was catty. Each of us went through our warm-ups methodically and almost grimly. I would imagine that the atmosphere before a battle must be like this, with each soldier alone with his or her thoughts, each in a separate world.

After my warm-ups, I looked up. The Pinecones and Chris had been allowed into the annex.

I went over to them.

"We just wanted to wish you good luck," said Darlene. "Then we'll get out of here."

Of all the Pinecones, I think Darlene knew best what I was going through. Big Beef has been in the Superbowl. Darlene knew all about pressure.

"You won't believe what the scalpers were offering us for our tickets," said Ti An. "A hundred thousand *pesetas*."

"It's a good thing that Lauren speaks Spanish," said Cindi. "She told them we wouldn't take a thousand dollars."

"We wouldn't take even that," said Ti An seriously.

"They *were* offering about a thousand dollars for four seats," said Lauren.

Ti An's mouth dropped open.

"We still wouldn't take it," said Jodi quickly.

"I never thought you would," I said. I glanced over at the floor mats. Patrick and Dimitri were arguing with one of the judges. I wondered what was going on.

"I've got to go," I said.

Jodi, Cindi, and Lauren looked reluctant to leave me, but Darlene picked up on my mood. "Come on, gang," she said. "We'll see Heidi on the winners' podium."

I looked Darlene in the eye. She knew how much winning meant to me.

"We still feel badly about that picture in *The Investigator*," said Cindi.

"It wasn't your fault," I said. "It was nobody's fault."

"It was *too* somebody's fault," argued Jodi. "The stupid reporter should never have printed those lies."

I laughed. Jodi's vehemence struck me as funny.

"You're right," I said. "It was his fault."

"Yeah, but if we hadn't gotten you to goof around, it would never have happened," said Lauren. "It distracted you when you didn't need any distractions."

"Maybe it was good for me," I said. "I had the

best practice in months yesterday."

"You mean maybe we did our job?" asked Cindi eagerly.

"What job?" I asked.

"Keeping you centered," said Cindi. I stared at her, remembering that was what I had said. It seemed like a long time ago. I don't think I would ever put it that way now.

"I liked having you here," I said. "But now, shoo."

"We'll be cheering," said Darlene as she herded the Pinecones out.

Chris gave me a hug. "Beat Nadia," he said.

" 'Gymnastics is a sport of the individual competing against no one but herself,' " I said, quoting one of the official mottos of the federation.

"Kick Nadia in the you know where," Chris repeated.

"Hey, Chris?" I asked him. "With our parents, how did you end up so . . . okay?"

"Practice, practice, practice," said Chris. I laughed. I gave him a hug.

I watched him leave with the Pinecones. Things had changed for me since I had arrived in Barcelona. I didn't think I would ever say something as gooey as "the Pinecones are my center" anymore. I was glad they had come, but now I just wanted to be alone to have a few minutes to concentrate before the finals.

But it wasn't to be. Mom, Dad, and Marshall had arrived in the annex. I blinked, hoping like a little kid that if I closed my eyes they would go away.

They came toward me. I tried to smile.

Dad gave me a hug. "One hug for good luck and then we're out of here," he said.

I looked up at him gratefully. At least he understood that I needed to be alone.

"How's the shoulder?" asked Marshall.

"It feels okay," I said.

"Good," he said. "You're a tough competitor. Good luck!" He didn't try to say any more. He shook my hand and went out into the main arena. I just wished that he had taken Mom with him.

"Are you sure you're all right?" she asked anxiously.

I rolled my shoulder in its socket. I had a full range of motion. "Yes," I said. I glanced up at the clock. There was less than an hour to go. I had to get rid of her.

"I'm sure that tabloid photograph preyed on your mind last night," said Mom.

I stared at her. Of all the things on my mind last night, the tabloid photograph hadn't come close. But to Mom that photograph was important. It was sad. But I couldn't help her.

"Having the Pinecones come to the Olympics was a mistake," said Mom.

"Andrea!" snapped Dad. "Hush up. Heidi doesn't need that from you right now."

Mom stared at Dad. He almost never spoke to her like that.

"That photo didn't matter, Mom," I tried to explain. "It's got nothing to do with reality."

"What do you mean?" Mom asked.

"Reality begins in less than an hour. It'll be me out there, not some image."

"The you that's out there can win," said Dad.

I nodded. "Thanks, Dad," I said. He hugged me a second time.

I turned to Mom. "Try not to fall again," she said. I couldn't believe her words. Poor Mom, she still didn't get it. Gymnastics was *not* about trying not to fall. Winning was about taking risks. If all I worried about was "not falling," I wouldn't even make it to the top ten. Trying to be perfect was very different from trying to win. Nobody ever won by not falling. It could never take you over the top.

24

Not One Inch

I hurried over to Dimitri and Patrick to get my final instructions. They both looked upset.

"The rotation!" sputtered Dimitri. "It's a fix. I know it."

"Calm down," Patrick hissed. "You're going to get yourself thrown out of here." He turned to me. "We've already argued with the judges, but they won't budge."

"What's wrong with the rotation?" I asked. The final competitors were going to be split into four different rotations. While one was on the beam, the others would be doing floor, vault, or bars. Usually, although no one likes to talk about it, the judges set the rotation so the top competitors have an advantage. Because my score had been so high in the compulsories and optionals, I should have been given a good rotation. The best rotation is one that allows you to go ahead early, to get a chance to do your best events when you're strongest.

"The Russian judge did this," Dimitri fumed.

I turned to Patrick. Obviously Dimitri was too furious to tell me. "What?" I demanded.

"The official word is that Nadia will do beam first."

"And me?" I asked. "When do I do bars?"

"It's the last on your rotation," said Patrick.

"She'll be ahead, first," said Dimitri. "You will have to fight all night long."

Dimitri bit his fingernail. I knew he was worried.

I shook my shoulders. There was nothing anybody could do about the rotation.

Suddenly there was a trumpet fanfare over the loudspeakers.

"The parade of the athletes will begin. Will the judges and coaches please leave the annex and go to the main arena?"

Dimitri gave me a pat on the back.

The Spanish gymnasts had been assigned the honor of being our guides. Melba was dressed in an all-white warm-up suit. She held up a sign with a vault on it. Vault would be my first event.

It was also the one for which I was least prepared after my injury.

Nadia went to stand behind the girl holding up the sign for the beam. She gave me a cool stare. I knew she thought she had me beat before the competition even began.

I rubbed my shoulder, begging it to hold up for just a little longer. Afterward I would give it all the rest it wanted.

We walked out into the Pavilion. I heard a rumbling roar, like a thunderstorm moving slowly through a valley in the mountains. The crowd was standing, cheering, and stamping their feet.

The beautiful glass Jordi Pavilion was packed. I looked up into the stands and all I could see was a sea of flags: American, Russian, Chinese, Kenyan, Argentinean, Japanese, Spanish, French . . . it was as if the stands had been turned into a huge undulating patchwork quilt.

The hair on the back of my neck felt as if it were standing straight up. I swallowed a lump in my throat and blinked.

I glanced over at Nadia, marching across from me. Her face was set in a tight mask, no emotion peeping through. She looked crisp and calm. Whatever tension she was feeling, she was managing to hide. There was no trace of doubt in her face.

We stayed at attention while they played the Spanish national anthem.

Then it was time to begin. I went over to the side by the vault and pulled off my warm-up suit.

"Just six minutes," said Dimitri. "Give me six minutes, ve have the vorld."

I knew what he meant. My entire performance, beam, vault, bars, my floor exercise, it all added up to no more than six minutes in front of the judges, six minutes of athletic, superhuman effort.

I heard another roar from the crowd. Nadia was beginning her beam routine.

"Don't vatch," said Dimitri.

But I couldn't take my eyes off her. She was like a queen taking the throne. There was not a single reckless move. She polished off hand springs, leaps, turns, and splits, as though the beam were as wide as the plaza in front of the Kremlin. Every part of her body added to her grace. Her neck was long and her shoulders loose. Even her fingertips were in perfect alignment. She was truly the embodiment of the cliché "poetry in motion."

Her dismount was a double back somersault. Nobody else could get the grace that Nadia could put into it.

Nadia knew she was stupendous the moment she touched the ground. She waved and threw kisses to the crowd.

The crowd went wild.

"It's a ten," I said to Dimitri and Patrick grimly.

Dimitri shook his head. "Nah, the judges give no tens in this Olympics."

I heard yet another roar. I looked back. Nadia had gotten the first 10 of the Olympics. She punched her fist into the air, the only un-Nadia-like movement I had ever seen her make.

If only gymnastics were like wrestling. I wished I could be like my Romanian friend and get Nadia into a hammer-lock and shove her face into the mats. In gymnastics you can never win like that. There is nothing I could do to *make* Nadia lose.

I wanted to be perfect in my vault. The vault I was doing was not nearly as daring as the one that I knew Nadia would do. My shoulder was just not strong enough.

I went to the runway and saluted the judges.

I ran full out. I hit the vault and felt the pain shoot up through my shoulder, but I ignored it, twisting high in the air. My knees came apart a little, although I landed it perfectly.

I stuck the landing!

Dimitri threw his fist into the air. It was the best vault I had done since the injury. We waited for the score.

The judges' scores came up. 9.8. The Russian judge had scored me low, but not low enough to risk a challenge. I bit my lip. I would just have to do better on my second vault.

"It's okay," I said to Dimitri, "I can do it." I felt calm, even though I was behind.

My second vault was even better than my first. I sailed over the horse, my body as tight as a board. I stretched my toes in alignment, and I knew it was beautiful. Except at the end I had too much power for the landing. I wound up doing a bunny hop forward.

The judges gave me a 9.6. The crowd booed, thinking my score was too low.

"Hey," said Dimitri, "it's going to be all right."

I wiped my face with a towel. I knew he didn't really believe it. Dimitri was giving up hope. A two-tenths deficit in the Olympics was like a football team being down by forty points. Nobody really believed that I could catch up.

Yet I felt so strong, even though I was behind.

It was time for my beam exercise. There was no room for error. If I fell now, there'd be no way I could catch Nadia. I frowned. Playing it safe was my mom's way. What had she told me? "Try not to fall." My mom's doubts couldn't touch me out here.

"You have to vork now like you have never vorked in your life. Okay? Never," said Dimitri.

I nodded. I would forget my mom.

My mount — a stag leap — was steady. My

turns were flawless. I flung my body into the air and dived down toward the beam. I could hear the crowd gasp as they thought I was falling, but I wasn't. I held out my hands and caught my weight. Some athletes say that at the height of competition, even when they're injured, they don't feel a thing.

That wasn't true. The pain was shooting up my arm into my shoulder, but I could ignore it. I flaired out my legs, holding all my weight with my arms. I kept my face still like a mask. No one would see my pain.

Then I flung myself back up onto the beam. More leaps now and all of them sure.

I nailed the dismount, my own double-back somersault. I hit the mats and held on. It was a rock-solid landing.

The air came whooshing out of me. I could hear Dimitri shout "Yah!" on the sidelines.

I was great! I flew over to Dimitri. He gave me a hug.

"Purrfect!" he shouted. "They have to give you a ten."

We waited anxiously for the score. When it came, 9.99, Dimitri groaned. I blinked. It had been the best routine of my life. It was a 10.

I watched as Nadia did a very safe bar routine. The judges gave her a 9.98, far higher than she deserved. Now the gold medal was almost out of sight for me.

The only way I could catch her would be to get two 10s on my last events, and so far the judges hadn't given me even one 10, no matter how spectacular I had been.

I could hear the television commentators on the sidelines. They were all saying that Nadia had it sewed up. "Heidi Ferguson has given it a game try, but with her sore shoulder she just doesn't have a chance," I heard one reporter whisper into her microphone.

I wanted to grab it and shove it down her throat.

I walked with my head held high over to the floor mats.

Dimitri took my face in his hands. "Nadia, she is all inside. But you . . . you can make that crowd fall in love with you. The judges will follow. Look at the people. Look at the faces. Smile. You've got to show it off. Show the judges."

I took a deep breath. I looked out into the crowd. I could hear a group screaming, "Hei-dee! Hei-dee! Hei-DEE!" I saw Darlene standing and shouting.

Below her I could see Mom, looking anxious. I forced my eyes back up a row. I locked onto the faces of the Pinecones.

Then I saluted the judges and took my pose on the floor.

My hands were high over my head. I started with a victory pose. It was an audacious way to start, but Dimitri had designed it for me. It announced to the world that I knew what I wanted.

I threw myself into my first tumbling pass. If I hit it, I knew I could do anything. It was a front flip, followed by four back handsprings, into a double somersault. It required me to fly over the space. I couldn't smile. I had to concentrate.

I charged myself, and blam, blam, blam — I hit each one.

The crowd roared. Now I could smile. I could hear Dimitri shouting at me, "Look at people! Look at people!" I locked on to the face of a little girl waving a Spanish flag in the front row. Then I turned, and looked straight up to the Pinecones.

It was as if all of time and motion had slowed down. I shouldn't have been able to pick out individual faces, but instead of a sea of thousands in the crowd, the entire 17,000 seemed to break apart into individuals for me. Strangers and friends, they were all with me. And it was all happening in that split second before my next move.

I landed my final pass with authority. The

167

warmth of the crowd's cheers enveloped me. Tears were streaming down my face. I couldn't stop them.

I ran to Dimitri and Patrick. They both had tears in their eyes, too. "No vay that von't get a ten," said Dimitri. "There is no vay. It is the best floor routine ever done. That is perfection."

The judges seemed to be taking forever. "Come onnnn," I begged them.

Then the numbers flashed on the board. Every judge had given me a 10 except the Russian judge, and even she had given me a 9.99. The crowd went wild.

"Yes!" I shrieked. Patrick nudged me back out onto the floor to acknowledge the crowd's applause. Dimitri was whooping like an Indian in an old-time western.

I heard the chants of "U-S-A! U-S-A!"

I came back and took a deep breath. It wasn't over yet. I had whittled Nadia's lead down to a five hundredths of a point.

It would all come down to Nadia's floor exercise and my bars. If she scored less than perfect, I could take her. Nadia passed me, her head held high. She wouldn't look at me.

I didn't blame her. We were locked in our own worlds now, she and I. The crowd couldn't help us in these final few seconds. Our teammates, friends, family, the commentators, even our coaches couldn't do it for us. Each of us was essentially alone. The tabloid photograph — Nadia's vanity — all of that didn't matter. We were two athletes who both wanted to win with every fiber of our beings. Neither of us would give an inch.

25

Only the Two of Us

Nadia had chosen music from *Carmen*, the song from the bullfight — the toreador's song. It was music that fit the mood of the arena in Barcelona like a glove, for she and I were like a matador and the bull, locked in a one-on-one battle. Only one of us could survive.

The crowd erupted when it heard the opening chords of the familiar song. The sound seemed to shake the rafters.

Dimitri didn't even bother to tell me not to watch. He was watching her too, and the truth is that I was glad that I didn't miss her. Every move flowed into the next, almost achingly beautiful, as if she were both the matador and the dying bull.

I knew it was a 10. I would have given her a 10 myself.

I took a deep breath. Her scores came up. I had been right. Every judge gave her a 10, but the Moroccan judge had given her a 9.9. Her routine's degree of difficulty had just not been as high as mine.

I had a chance. A very slim one. She was still .500 ahead. Nadia's rotation was over. All eyes would be on me.

The arena was strangely quiet, as if everyone had been exhausted by the emotion of our floor routines.

I went to the chalk bin and carefully dipped my hands into the chalk. I looked over at the bars.

Dimitri came over and stood beside me. "You do everything perfect — everything tight!"

"I'm doing the triple," I said.

Dimitri shook his head. "No, no, stupid. You do everything okay, they give you a ten vith the double. Everything in your routine is harder than vhat Nadia did. Don't need the triple."

"It's not a guaranteed ten," I said.

"But . . . you miss and *pffttt*."

Patrick came up to us. "Chie Watsuta is only one-tenth of a point behind you."

Dimitri exhaled all the air in his lungs. If I failed at the triple, I could lose to Chie, and Yang

Li wasn't that far behind Chie. A bad fall on my dismount could bring my score below 9. I wouldn't even get the bronze medal. The United States would get *no* medals in gymnastics.

And yet, if I landed the triple, the judges would have to give me a 10, even the Russian judge.

"I'm doing it," I said.

Dimitri swallowed hard. "Go for it," he said, without any trace of an accent. "You have nothing to lose."

Nobody needed to tell me that.

I took my position in front of the bars and saluted the judges.

"Control," I whispered to myself. "Control yourself up there. Swing and stretch. Do things longer." I took a second to check out my hand-grips — twice.

It was almost as if the 17,000 people in the arena, and the billion people they said were watching, were all holding their breath for me.

I looked up at the bars and took a deep breath. I had spent three-quarters of my life on those bars. They were home.

I arched into a perfect handstand. As I swung up over the high bar, I wanted to dominate every second that I was in the air.

Now, now, finally, there was no pain — it was just me, the bars, and the air. I owned the space around and above the bars.

As I got ready for my dismount, I sailed nearly twenty feet above the top bar. I twirled in midair, going faster than the naked eye could take in, and yet from inside my tight ball, everything was moving slowly — slower than any slow motion could ever catch. I felt as if I had an eternity to make my turns — once, twice, three times.

The crowd exploded when I got my feet under me. I hit the mats like a meteorite slamming into the earth. I planted my feet into the mats. I gripped with my toes as if there were raw earth under me. I willed myself not to let the momentum of my somersaults force me to my knees.

And I hung on.

I tossed my head back, drinking it all in.

I didn't realize that at that moment a photographer caught the total joy on my face.

"Ten, *Dix, Diez, Diez, Diez!*" The crowd screamed in English, Spanish, and seemingly all the languages of the world, yelling at the judges in a babble of languages to give me a perfect 10.

The judges' scores flashed on the screen: 10, 10, 10, 10, 10, 10.

I sank to my knees. I had done it.

Dimitri and Patrick surrounded me. I stood up.

Thousands of flashbulbs went off in my face, blinding me.

Nadia's coach had her arms around her, consoling her. Her head was down.

Then she brought her head up. Her eyes were wet, but not defeated. She saw me staring at her, and she nodded. We were each beyond words. Only the two of us knew what we had just been through.

26

Singing My Heart Out

The first words over the loudspeaker were in Spanish. I could pick out only my name. Then they repeated the announcement in French, the official language of the Olympics. I was really going to have to learn to speak another language.

Then, finally, the announcer repeated the words in English: "Winner of the gold medal, representing the United States of America, Heidi Ferguson."

A Gymnastics Federation official came forward with the gold medal and draped it around my neck. I couldn't believe how bright the gold was. It looked fake, it was just so — so — gold.

Nadia came over from the second-place level and gave me the customary kiss on both cheeks.

Her eyes were dry now. She said nothing.

Chie Watsuta tripped coming over from the third-place level. The crowd laughed. She kissed me. "You were incredible," she said in perfect English. I hugged her back.

Then a woman gave all three of us bouquets.

The announcer's voice came over the loudspeaker, "*Señoras y señores, levantarse por favor para el himno nacional de los Estados Unidos.*"

In the center of the arena, a giant red, white, and blue flag was pulled higher than the flag of the U.S.S.R. and of Japan.

I put my hand over my heart and belted out, "Oh, say can you see . . ."

I knew I was off key, but I didn't care. I had tears running down my cheeks that I could not stop.

I sang my heart out.

27

Gold Never Tarnishes

"Can't somebody tell the captain to get this plane moving?" I whined.

We were stuck on the runway. My gold medal was in a box in my knapsack. I had refused to wear it but, on the other hand, I had refused to let anybody else carry it.

"Relax," said Mom. She patted my hand. We were sitting in first class. Mom had convinced me that I needed to sleep on the plane, and for once, she made sense.

The last day of the Olympics had been almost more exhausting than the days of competition. I had spent half the night of my victory talking to the television networks. I had been chauffeured around Barcelona in a limousine going from press conference to press conference. I was sick of telling everybody how thrilled I was and of answering questions about anorexia and my shoulder. The closing ceremonies had been a blur. They felt like the last night of summer camp, a lot of tears, but already in our hearts the other athletes and I had begun to slip back into our own worlds. Some of us would never see each other again but, within our own sport, we knew that the next competition was just around the corner. It never ends until you get off.

I took out the gold medal and fingered it. I still couldn't get over how bright gold it was. Solid gold. It was heavy in my hand.

"It really is beautiful," said Mom. "It's almost a piece of art, a sculpture."

"Vonce you get a taste for the gold, watch out," teased Dimitri from across the aisle. He and Patrick had accepted Mom and Dad's invitation to fly first class with them. Dad was sitting with Marshall, sorting through the offers to make endorsements that I had received.

Chris was sitting next to Darlene in coach with the rest of the Pinecones.

"I'm so proud of you," said Mom. She was looking at my medal. "The gold is so gold."

I giggled. Mom looked at me. "What?" she

asked. I knew she thought I was laughing *at* her, but I wasn't.

"That's exactly what I thought when they handed it to me," I said.

"You'll have it the rest of your life," said Mom. "The wonderful thing about gold is that it never tarnishes." Mom sounded so serious, as if I really was worried about my having to polish my medal.

Finally, the pilot announced, "*Señoras y señores*, ladies and gentlemen we are ready for take-off."

"Finally," I sighed. I felt the power of the plane as we fought against gravity and won, the way I had. After all, what is gymnastics but a constant fight against gravity. I giggled again. I was in danger of taking myself much too seriously. I was in need of a dose of the Pinecones.

"Now what are you laughing at?" Mom asked.

"Nothing, Mom," I said.

"Do you want to look at your scrapbook?" Mom asked.

"Okay," I said. I didn't want to hurt her feelings. Mom handed it to me. It had the picture of me on the cover of *Hour* magazine. It was a close-up of me just at the moment when I had landed the triple. I stared at my image on the cover of the magazine. It was already seeming unreal, as if it had all happened to someone else.

"It's a great picture, isn't it?" I admitted.

"Yes," said Mom. "I'm arranging to get a blow-up of it for our living room."

"I'm not sure that I want to live with myself more than life-size," I said.

Mom looked annoyed.

"It's a joke, Mom, a joke." I fingered through the rest of the scrapbook. Mom had carefully edited out all the stories about anorexia. I guess some things would never change. The stewardess came down the aisle with a cart full of caviar. I hate little fish eggs.

The lighted seatbelt sign went off. I unbuckled mine.

"Where are you going?" Mom asked.

"I'm going to go check on the Pinecones," I said.

"I'm sure they are fine in coach," snapped Mom.

"Mom," I said, "I *want* to be with them."

"Let her go," said my father. He winked at me. "Want to leave your medal with us?"

"No way," I said.

I went back into coach. Lauren waved to me. There was an open seat between her and Jodi. Cindi, Ti An, and Ashley were right across the aisle. I plopped down into the empty seat.

Chris and Darlene leaned over the seat in back

of us. "Decided to come back here and party with the peasants?" teased Chris.

"Yeah," I said. "I never liked caviar much anyhow."

"So where's the medal?" asked Cindi. I patted my pocket and took it out again.

We all looked at it, in my lap. It glowed there. "For the rest of your life, everybody will always say, 'Heidi Ferguson, she won the gold,' " said Lauren. She sounded so awed, I wanted to laugh. And yet, I knew Lauren was being serious. The gold medal would be with me the rest of my life, no matter where I eventually put it. It would set me apart.

I looked at it again and then I put it away.

"So what have you guys been doing back here?" I asked.

"Oh, just some light reading," said Jodi. She took out the copy of *Hour* magazine.

"I think we bought up every copy in the airport," said Ti An, who was thumbing through the special sixteen-page section on the Olympics. "I'm putting this straight into my scrapbook."

"Oh, me too," said Lauren. "But I'm keeping this one too." Lauren pulled out the picture from *The Investigator* of me with my finger in my mouth.

I laughed. I remembered what Dr. Joe had said: "The Pinecones are friends, not crutches."

I took the tabloid picture from Lauren. "I'm gonna keep both pictures too," I said. I meant it. But the pictures were just for memories. I knew what was real. My gold medal was real. I had won. Winning was real, and it mattered. To me, the pictures could fade. The winning wouldn't. The gold would never fade either. Gold never tarnishes. I had wanted to laugh at Mom when she had said that, but she was right. I had won the gold.

About the Author

Elizabeth Levy decided that the only way she could write about gymnastics was to try it herself. Besides taking classes, she is involved with a group of young gymnasts near her home in New York City, and enjoys following their progress.

Elizabeth Levy's other Apple Paperbacks are *A Different Twist*, *The Computer That Said Steal Me*, and all the other books in THE GYMNASTS series.

She likes visiting schools to give talks and meet her readers. Kids love her presentation. Why? "I do a cartwheel!" says Levy. "At least I try to."

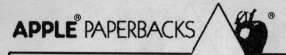

APPLE® PAPERBACKS

Pick an Apple and Polish Off Some Great Reading!

BEST-SELLING APPLE TITLES

☐ MT43944-8	**Afternoon of the Elves** Janet Taylor Lisle	$2.75
☐ MT43109-9	**Boys Are Yucko** Anna Grossnickle Hines	$2.75
☐ MT43473-X	**The Broccoli Tapes** Jan Slepian	$2.95
☐ MT42709-1	**Christina's Ghost** Betty Ren Wright	$2.75
☐ MT43461-6	**The Dollhouse Murders** Betty Ren Wright	$2.75
☐ MT43444-6	**Ghosts Beneath Our Feet** Betty Ren Wright	$2.75
☐ MT44351-8	**Help! I'm a Prisoner in the Library** Eth Clifford	$2.75
☐ MT44567-7	**Leah's Song** Eth Clifford	$2.75
☐ MT43618-X	**Me and Katie (The Pest)** Ann M. Martin	$2.75
☐ MT41529-8	**My Sister, The Creep** Candice F. Ransom	$2.75
☐ MT42883-7	**Sixth Grade Can Really Kill You** Barthe DeClements	$2.75
☐ MT40409-1	**Sixth Grade Secrets** Louis Sachar	$2.75
☐ MT42882-9	**Sixth Grade Sleepover** Eve Bunting	$2.75
☐ MT41732-0	**Too Many Murphys** Colleen O'Shaughnessy McKenna	$2.75

Available wherever you buy books, or use this order form.

Scholastic Inc., P.O. Box 7502, 2931 East McCarty Street, Jefferson City, MO 65102

Please send me the books I have checked above. I am enclosing $_____ (please add $2.00 to cover shipping and handling). Send check or money order — no cash or C.O.D.s please.

Name _____

Address _____

City_____ State/Zip _____

Please allow four to six weeks for delivery. Offer good in the U.S.A. only. Sorry, mail orders are not available to residents of Canada. Prices subject to change.

APP591